MUFFINS

M000012334

A Sandy Bay Cozy Mystery

By

Amber Crewes

Amber Crewes

Muffins and Coffins

Amber Crewes

Other books in the Sandy Bay Series

Muffins and Coffins

A

Sandy Bay

COZY MYSTERY

Book Thirteen

Amber Crewes

1

MEGHAN SMILED SLEEPILY as she awoke to the sound of birds chirping outside of her open bedroom windows. She sighed, inhaling the sweet, floral scent of the honey locust growing just below her second story apartment, thrilled that winter had finally ended and spring was making its first appearances in Sandy Bay, her adopted hometown in the Pacific Northwest.

Still enjoying the sounds of the morning, Meghan snuggled further beneath her comforter. She reached over and picked up Fiesta and Siesta, her tiny twin dogs, and piled them both on her chest. "Good morning, babies," Meghan murmured as she gave them each a kiss on the forehead. "It's finally the weekend. Your mama only works a few hours this morning, so perhaps we will go for a little walk on the beach later."

Meghan giggled as Siesta licked her on the nose. Fiesta followed suit, and Meghan scratched her behind the ears. She inhaled, and caught the smell of fresh muffins coming from the bakery downstairs.

"It smells like Trudy is off to a great start this morning," she said aloud, picturing her trusted middle-aged employee, Trudy, dressed in her apron and preparing the muffins. "She is such a rockstar on the morning shifts."

Meghan took another deep breath, detecting a hint of lavender as she closed her eyes. "I hope she is making the lemon-lavender muffins today. Those have been selling out like crazy."

Meghan lounged for a few more minutes, and then, as she heard Pamela, a local teenager she had hired a few months ago, greet Trudy downstairs, she peeled herself out of bed. She gathered her long, dark hair into a high ponytail and slipped into a pair of green cargo pants. She tied her apron on over her outfit and quickly surveyed herself in the mirror as she walked to her door. Meghan preferred a natural look; she typically did not wear a lot of makeup, and she smiled at her reflection as she passed the mirror.

At twenty-eight, Meghan felt more beautiful than ever, inside and out; she had raven-colored hair that fell down her back in soft waves, a light smattering of coffee-colored freckles across her small nose, and enormous dark eyes with long lashes. She was also the founder and owner of Truly Sweet, a bakery that had quickly gained popularity in its first year of business, and she was proud of the hard work that had turned the bakery into a massive success. Meghan also had a serious relationship with Jack, a detective, and she fell in love with him more and more every day. She had a good relationship with her family, who lived in Texas, and she had developed several meaningful, close friendships in Sandy Bay.

Everything had been falling in place for Meghan, and she was happier than ever. It would soon be her one-year anniversary of moving to Sandy Bay, and she was hoping to throw a party to celebrate. She had been weighing the idea for several weeks, and she was ready to share it with Trudy and Pamela. After brushing her teeth and applying a thin layer of lip gloss, Meghan walked downstairs and into the kitchen, excited to tell her employees about the party.

"Good morning, ladies," Meghan greeted them as she tucked a loose strand of dark hair back into her ponytail. "I have something I would like to share with you today!"

Pamela turned to Meghan, her nose wrinkled in disgust. She held out her phone to show Meghan the screen. "Does it have anything to do with this?"

Meghan peered at Pamela's phone. It was opened to the bakery's Instagram page. "Why are you showing me the Instagram page, Pamela? I told you that I liked the last few pictures you posted."

Pamela shook her head. "Look closer. I'm in the private messaging section."

Meghan squinted. "It's a message about a funeral service," she gasped. "They want to know if Truly Sweet sells coffins and provides funeral services."

Pamela nodded. "We've gotten five messages from different accounts this morning," she explained, her face filled with confusion. "When I message the accounts back, they vanish off of social media. It seems like a prank."

Trudy stepped forward, her arms crossed over her chest. "The same thing has been happening with our Facebook page," she told Meghan. "It's the strangest thing; we've been getting message after message about the bakery offering funeral services."

Meghan bit her bottom lip, feeling deflated. She had wanted to bring up the idea for the party, but now, it was evident that this issue needed to take priority over the celebration.

"What should we do, Meghan? Should we ask Jack to check this out?" Pamela asked earnestly. "He's a detective. He can track down whoever is pranking us."

Meghan laughed. "It doesn't seem like an emergency," she patiently said. "But, I will give Jack a call. This is starting to feel like harassment, especially if it is coming from two forms of social media."

Meghan pulled her phone out of her pocket and gasped as she unlocked the main screen. A chain of emails popped up, each with the subject line **FUNERAL SERVICES**.

"What is it?" Trudy asked, peering over Meghan's shoulder. "Oh no! It's the same thing. Why are people asking us for funeral services? We are a bakery."

Pamela's eyes grew wide. "I'm creeped out, Meghan," she told her boss. "Call Jack right now!"

Meghan paused for a moment, trying to make sense of the emails and messages. "Do you think someone is pulling an April Fool's Day prank?" she asked her employees. "I know it's a week past April Fool's, but what if…?"

Trudy pursed her lips. "I don't think so," she answered. "In Sandy Bay, no one really takes April Fool's Day seriously; I know they do some silly activities at the high school, but no one takes it too far."

"Yeah," Pamela agreed. "A couple of my friends left balloons and silly string in a locker, but no one would be rude to businesses in town. That would be so dumb."

Meghan cleared her phone screen and began dialing Jack's number, eager to hear his opinion on the matter. "Ugh, it went straight to Jack's voicemail. I'll have to call him later."

Trudy put her hands on her hips. "Well, we have about fifteen orders of muffins to fill before you are off for the afternoon," she informed Meghan. "Why don't we get started? Pamela and I will keep an eye on the social media pages for now, and you can pass along the word to Jack when you get ahold of him."

"That sounds good," Meghan agreed as she stepped over to the sink to wash her hands.

The three ladies baked two batches of muffins, trying to forget about the strange inquiries they had received. When the little silver bells attached to the front door chimed, Meghan sent Pamela out front. "Our first customer of the morning," Meghan said cheerfully as she shooed Pamela into the dining room. "Go wait on them, Pamela."

Pamela returned a moment later, her face pale and her hands shaking. "What is the matter?" Meghan asked, seeing the shock on her face.

"It's an old man," Pamela stammered. "And he asked if we sell *coffins*."

2

THE NEXT AFTERNOON, Meghan accompanied her friend, Karen Denton, to the fruit market. The weather was beautiful, and Meghan was delighted that some of the vendors had moved their stands outside. Meghan wore her favorite sunglasses, enjoying the warm air.

"It was so strange," Meghan explained as she browsed through a display of peaches. "I went out into the dining room to see what was going on, and the old man was just as confused as I was. He couldn't remember who had told him, but he swore that he had heard that Truly Sweet was doing funerals."

Karen raised an eyebrow. "That is utterly strange, Meghan. The entire situation is strange."

Meghan shrugged. "I haven't received any other communications about funerals since the man came into the bakery yesterday. Jack told me that it was probably just a prank, and that we shouldn't worry."

Karen shook her head. "What a silly prank to pull,"

she scoffed as she examined a plum. "In my seventy-three years, I have never heard of something so ridiculous."

Meghan smiled, as she did every time Karen reminded her of her age. At seventy-three years old, Karen had more energy than anyone Meghan knew, and she was in excellent shape. Karen frequently ran marathons, lifted weights, and was arguably the healthiest person in Sandy Bay.

"This is what I have been looking for!" Karen exclaimed as she held up a bright green apple from a straw bin. "I have a new juicer at home, and I've been dreaming of an apple-Carle smoothie."

"A juicer, huh?" Meghan asked. "Is it hard to use?"

Karen shook her head as she gathered ten apples into her paper sack. "Not at all; the fellow at the store told me it would only take a few minutes to make as much juice as you could ever want."

Meghan licked her lips, imagining fresh fruits and healthy ingredients to make delicious smoothies. She wondered if the bakery could sell smoothies; they already sold coffee and tea, and perhaps smoothies would appeal to a new demographic of customers.

"Excuse me!"

Meghan cringed as she accidentally walked right into Sally Sheridan, one of Sandy Bay's oldest and grumpiest residents. The contents of Mrs. Sheridan's purse spilled, and Meghan dove to collect the items.

"I'm so sorry, Mrs. Sheridan," Meghan apologized as she gathered Mrs. Sheridan's things. "I didn't see you."

"You are so clumsy, Meghan Truman," Mrs. Sheridan cackled as Meghan gave her back the purse. "I was standing right in front of you, and you walked right into me. I don't know how you manage to be such a clumsy girl."

Meghan shook her head. "I don't know either, Mrs. Sheridan. It's something I am working on," she admitted. "I hope you are having a good afternoon otherwise? This weather is so pleasant."

"It's too hot for my taste," she grumbled.

"But you said this winter was too cold," Karen replied playfully. "Aren't you happy that the sun came out?"

"It's too bright," Mrs. Sheridan declared. "It's either too hot, or too cold. Never just right."

"Nothing is ever just right for you, Sally Sheridan," Karen muttered under her breath as Meghan jabbed her in the ribs with her elbow.

"What was that?" Mrs. Sheridan squawked.

"Oh, nothing," Karen said as Meghan gave her a look.

"Well, I must be going. I am off to see my Auntie at the nursing home," Mrs. Sheridan informed them.

Meghan and Karen's jaws dropped in unison. "Your

Auntie?" Meghan asked. "You have an *Auntie*?"

Mrs. Sheridan narrowed her eyes. "Yes? She's my dad's sister, and she lives at the nursing home on Apple Street."

Meghan tried to regain her composure, but she was shocked that Mrs. Sheridan, whom she believed to be the oldest woman in Sandy Bay, could have an *Auntie*.

"We have spectacular genes in my family," Mrs. Sheridan stated. "My Auntie is nearly one hundred years old. I hope to live to that age myself."

"And I am sure you will," Meghan politely offered as Mrs. Sheridan smiled. "What is your Auntie's name?"

"Lucy," Mrs. Sheridan said. "Lucy Hudson. She was a teacher for over fifty years in Sandy Bay. Karen, I'm sure you knew her."

"I did know Mrs. Hudson," Karen confirmed. "I was her student. I didn't realize she was your aunt, or that she was still…. around."

"You mean alive," Mrs. Sheridan giggled. "She is alive and well. You should stop by and visit her sometime; I am sure that she would love it. Anyway, I am off to the fish market for some tilapia. Meghan, I might drop by tomorrow for some muffins. I think Auntie would like some."

"Sounds great," Meghan said as she waved goodbye.

"Ugh," Karen shuddered as Mrs. Sheridan hobbled away on her cane. "I didn't realize Lucy Hudson and Sally Sheridan were related, but now that I do know, it makes complete sense."

Meghan laughed. "What do you mean by that?"

Karen shook her head. "If you think Mrs. Sheridan is a crotchety old lady, you should meet her Auntie," Karen explained. "Lucy Hudson was the meanest teacher I ever had. She would yell and scream at her students, and if you were naughty, she would lock you up in a closet behind her classroom door."

"That can't be true," Meghan said. "You must be teasing me."

Karen's face paled. "I promise, I am not teasing," she whispered. "Once, Mrs. Hudson caught me chewing gum in class, and she dragged me by my collar to the closet. I had to stay in there all day."

Meghan's eyes widened. "There is no way," she whispered.

Karen nodded. "She was terrible, but all of us were too scared to tell our parents. After she retired, she and her husband lived in a mansion in Helvetia Hills; he was an investment banker, and they had a bunch of money. He died twenty years ago, so they must have put her in the nursing home then…"

Meghan could tell that Karen was upset. "I can't believe a teacher would do that," she murmured as she patted Karen on the shoulder. "I'm sorry you had to think about it."

Karen pasted a smile on her face. "It's all good. I don't live in the past. I live in the fabulousness of right now! Anyway, let's change the subject. I hear there is an amazing sale going on at Sparkle today. Any chance you want to check it out after we finish up here?"

Meghan wrinkled her nose. Karen had been so upset by the mention of Mrs. Sheridan's Auntie, and Meghan was brimming with curiosity. How could a schoolteacher, someone whose purpose was to help and teach children, be so cruel? Meghan tried to dismiss the thought as she and Karen continued shopping, but she could not stop thinking about Mrs. Hudson, the terrible teacher.

"What a family," Meghan thought as she pictured Mrs. Sheridan's Auntie. "I thought my family was silly at times, but it sounds like Mrs. Sheridan's family is quite the circus act."

3

MEGHAN GIGGLED AS JACK SPRAYED the hose in her direction. "Stop that," she cried as he continued to aim the water toward her face. "Jack, come on! We are here to wash the *dogs*, not *me*!"

Jack winked flirtatiously, and Meghan felt her heart flutter. Though they had been dating for the better part of a year, Meghan still had butterflies in her stomach when she saw Jack's handsome face. His bright blue eyes, blonde hair, and muscular build sent shivers down Meghan's spine, sometimes, when she least expected it. Today, the couple was trying out a new pet salon, and the sight of Jack in his drenched t-shirt was causing Meghan to blush.

"Okay, okay," he said playfully, putting down the hose and holding up his hands in a fake surrender. "We'll wash the dogs."

Meghan smiled. "I knew we should have picked the drop-off option," she teased. "We could have dropped all of the dogs off for the afternoon, and they would have been groomed and ready for us when we returned."

Jack shrugged. "That didn't sound like fun," he protested. "Washing the dogs ourselves sounded like a good date idea, and it saved us fifty bucks."

Meghan laughed. "I know you love saving money."

Jack's face darkened. "I hate that I have to even pay my hard-earned money to get my dog washed and groomed," he said flatly.

Meghan looked at Dash, Jack's dog. She reached down and scratched his belly. "Jack, the dogs deserve a little treat now and then," she insisted. "I know you would rather just hose Dash down at your place, but this is good for him. They even threw in a free nail-trimming and teeth-cleaning. You can't do that at home."

"Fair enough," Jack admitted as he picked up Fiesta and began to soap her ears. "This place *is* pretty nice."

"It is," Meghan said as she glanced around, admiring the gray tile floors and large picture windows. "Jackie recommended it. She said that her friend from beauty school got sick of doing human hair and switched to dogs."

"I'm sure dogs are easier clients to handle," he laughed as Fiesta licked his fingers. "Hey, speaking of difficult clients, how is the funeral business going, babe?"

Meghan frowned at her boyfriend. "That isn't funny, Jack."

The smile vanished from Jack's face. "I'm sorry, Meghan," he said, stepping forward to pull Meghan into his arms. "I was just making a joke."

"It isn't funny," she muttered, pushing away from Jack's embrace. "It was one thing to have the emails and messages on social media about the funeral business, but to have that old man come into my bakery and ask in person? That was too much. It isn't funny to me."

Jack reached for Meghan again. He pulled her close and kissed her on the forehead. "I'm sorry," he repeated as Meghan eventually leaned into the hug. "I know you've been riled up about it. I shouldn't have made the joke."

Meghan sighed, breathing in the familiar scent of Jack's cologne as she buried her face in his chest. "It's just so strange," she lamented. "I don't know enough about the internet or social media to solve this mystery, and I don't know what I am going to do if it continues."

"Leave it to me. I will make sure that this doesn't turn into an issue," Jack assured her as he gently stroked her hair. "Your job is to run that bakery like the champ that you are, and to let me know if anything else comes up. Have you heard anything else since that man came into the shop?"

Meghan shook her head. "No," she told him. "Nothing. We've been monitoring all of our accounts, and I have been reading every message and email."

"Excellent," he said. "I am keeping an eye on things as well. You just keep me in the loop, Meghan, and I will take care of you. I'm having some of the police officers monitor the bakery, and Molly, our IT specialist at the station, is running some reports on your social media accounts."

"That's great, honey," she said. "Thank you for making those arrangements."

"Of course," Jack whispered as he leaned down to kiss Meghan's cheek. "You're my girl, Meghan. I want to keep you safe. My suspicion is that this whole thing is a prank, or worse, some kind of money scam. Just make sure you are watching your bank accounts, and if someone strange asks you for money, let me know."

The couple jumped apart quickly as Dash shook his body, spraying them with water and soaking Meghan's hair. "Not my hair," she cried, patting the bandana that had been holding back her long, dark locks. "I just washed it yesterday! Dash, why did you have to shake out all of the water on us?"

Jack struggled to hold back his laughter. "Didn't someone just say that the pets deserve a treat? Well, I guess Dash also deserved a laugh."

Meghan smiled in spite of herself. She reached for the damp blue towel hanging from the rack and pulled the soggy bandana out of her hair. "Our dogs sure keep us on our toes, don't they?"

Jack grinned, and suddenly, there was a knock at the

door. Through the window in the door, Meghan could see it was a tall, thin woman with long black hair. Meghan opened the door. "Hi," she said.

"Hello!" the woman greeted them as she stepped into the room. "I'm Hilda, the owner."

"Oh, so you know my friend, Jackie," Meghan replied in delight. "She said you went to beauty school together."

"We did," Hilda nodded. "How are you enjoying *Woof*? It's my first venture into a pet salon, but given how nasty people can be sometimes, it seemed like an easier business than the hair salon I used to run."

Meghan smiled warmly. "Woof is just adorable," she told Hilda. "We've loved the self-service option for the dogs, right babe?"

Jack nodded politely. "It's a nice setup," he agreed.

Hilda grinned, revealing jagged teeth that shocked Meghan. "I'm glad to hear it," she said as she produced a folder from her apron. "I wanted to introduce myself and drop off the bill. The payment information is inside. Thank you, and enjoy the rest of your visit."

Jack and Meghan waved goodbye, and Jack reached for the folder. "Let's see the damage," he said. "It can't be too much, especially since we washed the dogs ourselves…"

Meghan watched as Jack's eyes nearly bulged out of

his face as he examined the bill. "Its three-hundred dollars," he yelped as Meghan bit her lip. "We washed the dogs ourselves! This can't be right…"

Meghan put a hand on Jack's shoulder. "I should have known it would be expensive," she admitted as she pried the bill from his hands. "Jackie mentioned that Hilda was an upscale kind of gal. Look, let me take care of the bill. It's no big deal, Jack, and I was happy to pamper the pups."

Jack shook his head. "It's okay," he said as he took a deep breath. "It's fine, really. Let's just say that this is the last time we will be coming to Woof. Grooming a dog is not worth this kind of money."

Meghan looked over and saw a face in the window. Hilda had returned to the door. Her face was dark, and her eyes were burning with hatred as she stared at Jack from the hallway. It was clear that she had overheard Jack's rant.

"Uh oh," Meghan gulped as she watched Hilda turn and stomp away.

Jack's face paled. "Uh oh is right," he said as he watched Hilda storm away from their self-cleaning cubicle.

4

"THERE, DO IT LIKE THAT, Pamela. If you hold the spoon like that, you'll be able to create the perfect swirls of icing," Meghan coaxed her young employee as they finished preparing an order of cupcakes.

"You do it so nicely," Pamela responded as Meghan swirled the red icing atop the vanilla cupcake. "How did you learn to do it so perfectly?"

Meghan laughed. "It's not perfect, but I practiced my icing abilities for a few months before I felt confident enough to sell my cupcakes. If you keep practicing, I know you will get the hang of it, Pamela. You are a natural in the kitchen, that's for sure."

Pamela grinned. She flipped the spoon to mirror the way Meghan was holding hers, and she began to ice a fresh cupcake. "Good!" Meghan praised her. "Just like that."

Suddenly, Trudy burst into the kitchen. "Meghan? Do we have a corporate order that is finished? A young woman from the Governor's office is here to pick it up, and to be honest, I have no idea what she is talking about."

Meghan smiled reassuringly at Trudy. "It's done," she kindly informed her employee. "We had a relatively small order for two dozen muffins. I decided to just knock them out myself early this morning; Siesta woke me up at 4:30 to go outside, and I just stayed awake and was productive the rest of the morning."

Trudy sighed in relief. "I am so happy to hear that. My heart was pounding when she called! I thought we had somehow missed the order."

Meghan shook her head. "We're old pros," she said, feigning haughtiness. "We've got this!"

Trudy nodded. "The young woman on the phone told me she would be by in a half hour to pick up the muffins."

Meghan gestured at Pamela. "Will you check the boxes and the wrapping? I want to make sure everything looks nice."

Pamela smiled and went to fetch the box of muffins, and a few minutes later, the little silver bells chimed. A statuesque woman dressed in a knee-length gray dress marched into the bakery, still talking into her cell phone as she approached the counter.

"Yes, I have a few more errands to run, and then I will be back. Have her secretary call mine, and I will make the arrangements. Thanks, ciao."

Meghan smiled as the woman nodded at her. "I'm here to pick up the order for the Governor's office," the woman informed Meghan.

"No problem," she replied. "Two dozen *matcha* muffins?"

"That's what I ordered," the woman said arrogantly.

Meghan was annoyed by the woman's rudeness, but she went to the back and retrieved the muffins, a smile still pasted on her face as she handed them to the governor's aid. "Here you are."

"I hope this is the last muffin run I do for him," the woman muttered under her breath.

"Excuse me?"

"The governor's weight is going up, and his constant talk of diets and exercise routines is getting old," the woman told Meghan as she pulled out a compact from her purse and examined her reflection. "I hope his doctor bans him from sweets so I can stop making these trips. It takes me an hour to come all the way here, get the muffins, and get back to the office. It's so annoying."

Meghan wrinkled her nose. "Sorry to be an inconvenience," she shrugged.

"No problem," the woman snarkily answered. "See you later."

Meghan shook her head as the rude woman strutted

out. "People can be so rude," she lamented as she watched the woman slide into her sleek gray sports car.

"People can be the worst!"

Meghan looked over and saw Mrs. Sheridan hobble into the bakery. "How are you today, Mrs. Sheridan?" she asked politely.

"Just the usual, Meghan. I need to make a return."

Meghan stifled a shudder; Mrs. Sheridan was notorious in Sandy Bay for trying to return anything and everything she bought, including already-consumed food, clothing, pets, vehicles, kitchenware, and more.

"I bought a box of your muffins last week," Mrs. Sheridan began as Meghan bit her lip. "I've eaten five out of the six muffins, and they were actually decent, but the sixth muffin…"

Meghan raised an eyebrow. "What was wrong with the sixth muffin?"

Mrs. Sheridan frowned. "It was smaller than the others."

Meghan wrinkled her nose. "Well, did you bring it back? If it was smaller than the others, I'm happy to exchange it for a larger muffin."

Mrs. Sheridan reached into her bulky faux crocodile skin purse and pulled out a crumpled piece of yellow tissue, the same paper that Meghan used to stuff in the boxes of muffins. "Well, I already ate it, of course; it was a decent muffin as well, but just small. I brought this tissue paper back as proof of my purchase."

Meghan silently reached into the display case and grabbed the largest muffin available. She wrapped it in yellow tissue paper, placed it in a box, and tied a yellow silk ribbon around it. "There," she said as she gave the box to Mrs. Sheridan. "Consider this your replacement."

Mrs. Sheridan grinned. "Thank you for understanding. People in town can get so fussy when I make my returns, but you are usually fairly reasonable."

Meghan nodded stiffly, still annoyed by the rude woman and now, irritated by Mrs. Sheridan. "No worries," she told Mrs. Sheridan. "Have a nice day."

"I'm not done yet," Mrs. Sheridan told Meghan as she pointed at the display case. "I would like to pack up a few more of the muffins; I want to take a few to my Auntie. She isn't allowed to have sweets, but she's so old, I don't think it matters."

Meghan dutifully plucked five muffins from the case and wrapped them up. "I can't believe someone as old as you can even have an elderly aunt," she murmured as she folded yellow tissue paper into the box.

"Excuse me?"

Meghan's heart sank; Mrs. Sheridan must have heard her comment. She could see Pamela and Trudy out of the corner of her eye, and they looked just as alarmed as she did.

"I was just talking to myself," Meghan claimed as she secured the yellow silk bow around the box.

"My Auntie will love the muffins," Mrs. Sheridan cooed as Meghan sighed in relief. "She is a wonderful woman. When I was a girl, my parents were always away on business trips; my father was an international attorney, and my mother was a diplomat. I hardly saw them, and if it weren't for my Auntie, I would have been raised by nannies."

Meghan smiled. "It's always nice to have the support of your family."

"It is," she agreed. "My Auntie wasn't everyone's cup of tea, but she taught me the discipline I needed. She loved me more than my parents, I think, and I owe her everything."

Meghan gently slid the box to Mrs. Sheridan. "I hope she enjoys these muffins, Mrs. Sheridan. She sounds like quite an…. interesting lady."

A loud, tinny sound began to ring through the bakery. Confused, Meghan looked to Trudy. "Trudy? What is that?"

"It sounds like a cell phone," Trudy answered. "I don't have one. I only have a pager. Pamela?"

Pamela shook her head. "My ringtone is the soundtrack from Hamilton. Meghan? Is that yours?"

"Nope. My ringtone is the sound of birds chirping. It must be…."

Everyone looked at Mrs. Sheridan, who seemed oblivious to the ringing. "What's going on?" she squawked. "Sorry, sometimes I am hard of hearing."

"Your phone?" Meghan said, maneuvering her hand to resemble a phone and holding it up to her ear. "I think your cell phone is ringing."

Mrs. Sheridan reached into her purse and retrieved a large, bulky cell phone. "Hello? Hello?"

Meghan watched as the color drained from Mrs. Sheridan's face. She dropped the cell phone and collapsed onto the bakery floor. "Mrs. Sheridan?" Meghan cried, rushing to the old woman's side. "What is the matter?"

Mrs. Sheridan was shaking. "My Auntie," she moaned. "She's *dead*!"

5

MEGHAN STARED IN SHOCK as Mrs. Sheridan wailed. She had never seen Mrs. Sheridan so upset before, and she kneeled down beside her and began gently stroking her back. "I am so sorry for your loss, Mrs. Sheridan," she whispered as Mrs. Sheridan cried. "Let us take you home; Pamela can mind the store, and Trudy and I will drive you. I am sure you are in shock and need to rest."

Mrs. Sheridan gasped. "I cannot go home," she declared. "I have to pay my respects immediately! My Auntie deserves to be honored, and I must go to the nursing home *now*."

Meghan furrowed her brow. "I'm not sure that is the best idea," she said softly. "Why don't we take you home for a bit? This is so tragic, but I think some rest would be good."

"I AM NOT GOING TO REST!" Mrs. Sheridan screeched as she pulled herself up off of the wooden floor. "My Auntie was my biggest role model, and I *will* go to the nursing home and pay my respects. Now, Trudy? Call a cab for me. I am going to the nursing home *right now*."

Meghan shook her head. "Don't bother with a cab," she told Mrs. Sheridan. "Trudy and I will just drive you there now."

Mrs. Sheridan nodded. "Let's go."

The three women escorted Mrs. Sheridan to Trudy's little blue Ford Taurus and sped off toward the nursing home. When they arrived, Mrs. Sheridan barreled past the security guard outside. "I'm family!" she screamed as she dashed inside.

Meghan and Trudy checked in with the guard and proceeded inside. "This is a nice nursing home," Trudy whispered to Meghan as they glanced around the foyer. "When we put my pop in a nursing home, it felt more like a morgue. This place is palatial."

Meghan agreed. With the shiny wooden floors, soft music playing, and diverse array of floral arrangements placed on bamboo tables, the nursing home felt like an opulent spa.

"Mrs. Sheridan."

The three women turned to see a short middle-aged woman approaching them. She had silver hair piled atop her head in an elegant bun, and she was dressed in a burgundy smock with black velvet leggings beneath. Her face looked concerned, and she ran to Mrs. Sheridan and wrapped her arms around her.

"Sally Sheridan, I am so, so sorry to hear about Mrs.

Hudson," the woman cooed as she embraced Mrs. Sheridan. "Mrs. Hudson was a wonderful woman, and we are going to miss her here."

Mrs. Sheridan wiped a tear from her eyes. "Thank you for the kind words, Valerie," she sniffled as the woman patted her back. "These are my friends, Meghan and Trudy. They accompanied me here. They were there when I heard the news."

The woman turned to Meghan and Trudy. "I'm Valerie Hodge," she told them with a soft smile, reaching out her hand to shake theirs. "Director of this facility. I have been working here in different capacities for over twenty years, and I knew Mrs. Hudson well. I was so sad to hear of her passing."

Meghan shook her hand. "It's nice to meet you," she said. "Although, I wish it were under better circumstances."

Valerie smiled sympathetically. "It happens," she said. "All too often in a nursing home, it seems, but we get used to it."

Mrs. Sheridan wiped a tear from her eyes. "Did you see her before it happened, Valerie?"

Valerie nodded sweetly. "I did," she cooed, placing a hand on Mrs. Sheridan's elbow and squeezing gently. "We chatted this morning during our buffet luncheon. She was in good spirits."

Mrs. Sheridan wiped her nose on her sleeve. "She was in good spirits when I saw her yesterday. She looked vibrant and seemed full of energy. I just don't understand how she could be doing so well yesterday and be dead today!"

Valerie leaned in toward Trudy, Meghan, and Mrs. Sheridan. "She was in happy spirits this morning," she began. "But there *was* something odd I noticed late last night," she murmured, looking over her shoulder to see if anyone was listening. "One of our nursemaids was ill last night, so I stepped in to do the last rounds of the evening."

Meghan raised an eyebrow. "So you saw something during the rounds?"

Valerie bit her lip. "Not something. *Someone.*"

Mrs. Sheridan's face grew dark. "Some*one*? Who? Auntie doesn't have visitors, except for *me.*"

Valerie clasped her hands together and inhaled. "It was Mark Tilley," she said as Mrs. Sheridan's jaw dropped. "I saw Mark Tilley coming out of her room last night."

Mrs. Sheridan's face turned white, and before Meghan could catch her, she fell to the floor, hitting her head and losing consciousness.

6

"WE COULDN'T WAKE HER UP. We had to call an ambulance," Meghan said gravely as she recounted the events of the previous evening to Karen, as well as her friend, Jackie.

"That's awful," Jackie murmured, pushing her newly-dyed jet-black hair out of her eyes. "So who was this Mark Tilley guy? Is it someone she knew?"

"Clearly!" Karen chimed in as she sipped her green tea latte. "She passed out! Meghan, tell us, who was he?"

Meghan took a bite of her warm chocolate chip cookie. The ladies had met up for an afternoon snack at *Moon Dollar*, a new coffee shop in the next town. Jackie had insisted making the trip, saying that she needed to get out of town for the day.

"Valerie wouldn't tell us," Meghan shrugged as she licked a piece of chocolate from the corner of her lips. "She was freaking out; Mrs. Sheridan's body was shaking uncontrollably after she passed out, and Valerie was losing her cool."

"That seems odd to me," Karen replied as she leaned against her yellow leather chair in the corner of the coffee shop. "She works at a nursing home. Surely people are passing out all of the time, no?"

Meghan bit her lip. "It isn't your average nursing home," she explained. "The place looks like a palace; there are high ceilings, famous works of art on display, and windows the size of this coffee shop overlooking a serenity garden that could put Luxembourg Garden in Paris to shame. I did some research after I got home last night, and from what I can tell, it costs a fortune to spend even one *night* there, let alone *years*! And, from the looks of her, it seems like Valerie isn't doing the dirty work there, so I'm not surprised she had such a strong reaction to Mrs. Sheridan's collapse."

Jackie shook her head. "Can you imagine having so much money?" she sighed. "Some of my clients at my beauty salon come in dripping with diamonds and wearing designer clothing, and I can only imagine what it's like to have that kind of dough."

Karen rolled her eyes. "Money is not everything," she insisted as she took another sip of her tea. "Health is what truly matters; you can have all of the money in the world, but if you don't have your health, what's the point?"

Jackie laughed. "I would choose millions of dollars over my health any day," she announced playfully as Karen scoffed. "I still want to know who that Mark Tilley is, though. I wonder if he killed Mrs. Hudson?"

Karen leaned in and clasped her hands together in a conspiratorial fashion. "I know who Mark Tilley is," she whispered, looking from Jackie to Meghan.

"You do?" Meghan cried.

"I do," Karen confirmed. "Mark Tilley and I went to grade school together; he was a few years younger than me, but we played on the same youth basketball team when we were children."

Meghan gasped. "Who is he?"

Karen took a deep breath. "He is Mrs. Hudson's nephew."

Meghan's dark eyes widened, and she clutched her heart. "You have to be kidding me."

Karen shook her head. "I'm not," she insisted. "Anyone who has lived in Sandy Bay for over forty years would know Mark Tilley; he is second cousins with Mrs. Sheridan."

"So they definitely know each other?" Jackie asked.

"Oh yes," Karen agreed. "They absolutely know each other; Mark Tilley is a notorious recluse, and he committed crimes that burned his name into the history of this town. Twenty years ago, he was convicted of operating an illegal dog-fighting ring just south of town. It was humiliating for the family; Mrs. Sheridan's grandparents were mortified, and they all cut ties with Mark."

"What happened next?" Meghan asked.

"He vanished," Karen said simply. "He was cast out of the family, and he went off the radar. A few years ago, his conviction was appealed and overturned by some technicality, but he stayed away from Sandy Bay society. His dream as a boy had been to open Sandy Bay's first zoo, but the original conviction prohibited him from working with animals in any capacity. I always kind of thought he would try to open a zoo after his conviction was overturned, but no. He has always stayed away..."

Meghan frowned. "A dog fighting business sounds terrible," she said. "But being cut off from your family? That's just cruel."

Karen nodded. "I agree," she told Meghan. "I think what those people did to Mark drove him off the edge. His entire family turned their backs when he was arrested, and he was never the same. Well, almost the entire family. He kept in contact with Mrs. Hudson."

Jackie wrinkled her nose. "Why would Mrs. Hudson stay in contact with her hoodlum nephew? Wasn't she supposed to be strict?"

"For some reason, she supported him financially after his incident," Karen murmured. "No one knew why, but everyone knew that once a year, Mark Tilley would show his face at the local bank, withdrawing thousands of dollars from Mrs. Hudson's account."

Meghan tried to make sense of Karen's story. "I just

don't understand," she said. "Why would she support him? Wouldn't she want to save face like the rest of her family?"

"They had always been close," Karen explained. "Mrs. Hudson's own son, Bobby, died in a freak canoeing accident before Mark was even born. Everyone always said that Mark was the spitting image of his deceased cousin, and from what I've heard, Mrs. Hudson took an interest in the boy when he was young. She was devastated by the news of his criminal activity, but she could not bear to say goodbye to the nephew who reminded her of her own son. She adored Mark, and he loved her back. They remained close until..."

Meghan slumped back in her orange leather armchair. "That is quite the story," she declared as she put her feet up on the little wooden coffee table below her seat. "But if Mrs. Hudson and Mark were so close, why would he kill her? She supported him financially. He wouldn't have any need to kill her."

Karen's face grew grim. "Mrs. Hudson's fortune is massive," she told them. "Whoever inherited her wealth would instantly become a millionaire...maybe a billionaire. Mrs. Hudson was not an easy woman to please. I wonder if Mark had disobeyed her, or had been cut out of the will? That would have given him a good reason to….do what he did."

Meghan's face darkened. "I think that's too much speculation," she scolded Karen. "The coroner hasn't even released a report on her death. Mrs. Hudson was one of the oldest women in the Pacific Northwest. It sounds like she was quite the force to be reckoned with, but perhaps she was just an elderly woman who passed away of natural causes."

Karen chuckled. "Oh, Meghan," she sighed as she reached over and patted Meghan's knee. "Mrs. Sheridan, Mrs. Hudson, and Mark Tilley are some of the most complicated people in this entire town. Mark my words, if Mrs. Hudson actually died of natural causes, it will be the most shocking thing I have ever heard. There's no way that Mark Tilley didn't have *something* to do with it. That creep has always been up to no good, and it sounds like he just did away with the only person who ever truly loved him."

7

MEGHAN PUSHED OPEN the yellow front doors of the bakery, enjoying the chime of the little silver bells as she walked inside. She was exhausted from the outing with Karen and Jackie, but despite feeling tired, she had to get back to work. Meghan made herself a fresh cup of coffee, drank it quickly, and went into the kitchen.

"You're back!" Pamela exclaimed as Meghan walked into the kitchen. "How was your coffee date?"

Meghan sighed. "It was fine," she answered wearily as she tied her yellow apron around her waist. "Anything major happen since I have been away?"

Pamela shook her head. "Nope, nothing crazy. Mrs. Sheridan called a few minutes ago."

Meghan stopped in her tracks, her dark eyes widening. She was still reeling from the intense conversation she'd had with her friends, and the last thing she wanted to do was talk with Mrs. Sheridan. "What did she want?"

Pamela smiled. "She just wanted to thank you for taking her to the nursing home," she explained as Meghan sighed in relief. "She would also like some muffins. I told her she would have to talk to you; I know how bad she is about returning *everything*, and I didn't want to deal with her coming in and out five times while you were out."

Meghan wrapped an arm around Pamela's thin shoulder. "You are sweet for being so protective of this bakery," she told her young employee. "But next time, I need you to sell the customers what they want, regardless of their history with us. Mrs. Sheridan just lost her dear Aunt, and she is quite upset. I think she deserves a few muffins to help her get through this difficult time."

Pamela's hands flew to her face, which was turning red as she looked in horror at Meghan. "I didn't even think of that," she whispered as her eyes filled with tears. "Meghan, I was snippy with her on the phone. I am so embarrassed. I think I need to go over to her house right away with a basket of hot, fresh muffins."

Meghan gave Pamela a quick hug. "We all make mistakes," she told the girl. "Did she seem upset when you refused her?"

Pamela bit her lip. "She definitely wasn't happy. Oh, Meghan. How could I have been so stupid? How could I have forgotten what's happening with her family?"

Meghan looked Pamela in the eyes. "Take a breath," she said calmly. "It happens. Things happen. We'll fix this, don't you worry."

Pamela ran for the display case and began to collect a sack of muffins. "I'll take her some blueberry ones, some red velvet muffins, and maybe the pear caramel? That's been one of our best sellers."

Meghan gently took the sack of muffins from Pamela. "Why don't you let me deliver these? I can run over to Mrs. Sheridan's, drop off the muffins, and be back before you know it?"

Pamela smiled weakly. "That sounds good," she told Meghan. "I'm too scared and embarrassed to face her right now after how much of an attitude I gave her."

Meghan laughed. "Oh, I wouldn't worry too much about your attitude," she told Pamela. "I'm sure Mrs. Sheridan gave it right back to you."

Meghan wrapped the muffins in a new box. She even wrote a card to go along with the arrangement, and she carefully slipped it beneath the yellow silk ribbon she had tied around the box.

Mrs. Sheridan,

We at Truly Sweet are so sorry for your loss. Please consider these muffins a token of our affection for you. We hope that they sweeten this sour time. Please do not hesitate to reach out if you need anything at all!

With love,
Meghan, Trudy, and Pamela

"What do you think?" Meghan asked Pamela. "I think the card is a nice touch."

"It is," she agreed. "I feel better now. I think she'll like the muffins and the card."

Meghan packed up her things and removed her apron. As she turned to leave the kitchen, Trudy walked in, her face grave. "What's wrong?" Meghan asked.

Trudy gulped. "We received another call about coffins," she said quietly. "I couldn't tell if the caller was a man or a woman, but when I asked who they were, they hung up the phone immediately. It was strange, to say the least."

Meghan's chest grew tight, and she felt her palms grow sweaty. Who was continuing to harass them about the funeral services? Why was the bakery being targeted? Was this some sort of prank, a mistake, or something much more sinister?

"Oh, Meghan," Pamela called out as Meghan walked out of the kitchen. "Mrs. Sheridan called from the nursing home, not her house. Just thought I would let you know."

When Meghan arrived at the nursing home, she checked in with the security guard, who then escorted her into the foyer. She was met by Valerie Hodge, who greeted her with a warm smile.

"Meghan," Valerie called out cheerfully as she leaned in and kissed Meghan on both cheeks. "How are you doing today?"

Meghan smiled weakly. "I'm doing alright," she told Valerie. "Is Mrs. Sheridan still here?"

Valerie's face fell. "She is, that poor dear," she clucked. "She insisted that she stay in her Auntie's room. She is so upset. Thank you for being such a rock for her, Meghan. Mrs. Sheridan mentioned that you were one of her dearest friends."

Meghan's heart warmed. Mrs. Sheridan was notoriously grumpy and rude, and while Meghan knew Mrs. Sheridan had warmed to her, she had not realized that Mrs. Sheridan considered her a close friend.

"It's heartbreaking to watch our residents' families go through their journey of grief as their loved ones pass away," Valerie continued. "But I love my job. It is so fulfilling to make the last days of these wonderful elderly people as peaceful and luxurious as we can. I feel more like the director of a spa, or a cruise activity director than a nursing home manager. While our residents are old, they sure do have a lot of zest for life, and I love that."

Meghan smiled. "It sounds like this is the perfect job for you," she told Valerie.

"It is," she agreed. "Managing *Sevenoaks* is what I was meant to do."

Meghan gestured at the box of muffins she was holding. "That's how I feel about my bakery," she explained. "It's what I was born to do."

Valerie eyed the muffins leerily. "You made those?" she asked as Meghan nodded. "Here at Sevenoaks, our residents' meals are prepared by top chefs. We don't allow gluten, sugar, wheat, dairy, or red meat on the premises. Surely you understand."

Meghan laughed. "Well, luckily, these aren't for your residents," she informed Valerie. "I brought these for Mrs. Sheridan. I know they aren't allowed here, but perhaps you could make an exception, especially since her Auntie just passed away?"

Valerie paused, but then nodded. "Of course," she agreed. "Now, let me show you to Mrs. Hudson's rooms."

Valerie led Meghan down a long hallway and paused in front of a set of doors. The doors opened to reveal an elevator with a uniformed attendant standing in the corner. "Fifth floor, please," Valerie instructed as the uniformed woman nodded and pushed the button. Meghan looked up at the mirrored ceiling, and seeing that her long, dark hair looked messy, she pulled it into a messy bun.

The doors opened, and Valerie led Meghan. The hallway was brightly-lit, with chandeliers hanging from the ceiling every few feet. The carpet was thick and red, and the walls were painted a soft eggshell color. As they walked, Meghan noticed there were no residents out of their rooms. This seemed odd to her, and she decided to ask Valerie some questions.

"Valerie, can I ask you a question?" Meghan asked. "Where are all of the residents?"

Valerie smiled. "Our residents' suites are quite spacious," she explained as she stopped before a tall mahogany door. "Most of our residents prefer to spend time in their rooms."

"Aren't there activities or games? What about meals? Do they eat in a dining room?"

Valerie laughed out loud. "Of course not. This is not a high school. There is no cafeteria. The residents are served their meals privately. They are of course welcome to spend time in the common spaces--the movie theater, spa, private art collection, and library are available at all times--but they tend to keep to themselves."

Meghan raised an eyebrow. "It sounds like a....unique place," she said.

"It's very special," Valerie glowed. "We adore our residents, and we hope the feeling is mutual."

"Speaking of your residents," Meghan started. "Mrs. Hudson? What did they determine as the cause of her death?"

Valerie shook her head. "That's private information," she said apologetically. "I'm sure you can ask Mrs. Sheridan, though. I believe she has the coroner's report by now."

Meghan nodded. "Of course. One more question? I'm just concerned about Mrs. Sheridan, and I want to make sure she has the best support during this difficult time."

Valerie smiled. "You are such a lovely friend to her."

"I try to be," she said modestly. "I know that she considers me a dear friend, but what about her family? I've heard that Mark Tilley is technically a cousin?"

Valerie's face darkened. "Mrs. Sheridan wants nothing to do with that man," she stated firmly. "Nor do I. I remember what he did to those precious dogs all those years ago, and I have never forgiven him. Are you a dog person?"

"I have two," Meghan told her.

"Then you understand," she declared. "That monster ran his ring of dog-fights, which is cruel. It also attracted the worst crowds to our town. I hated that he was allowed to visit Sevenoaks, but Mrs. Hudson adored him, for whatever reason...I always thought he still looked shady. He just has this bad look about him. I wanted to ban him from the property; we have swans outside in our pond, and that monster should not be around animals! Mrs. Hudson forbade it, though, and he was allowed to visit her as he pleased."

"You said you saw him leave her suite the night before she died," Meghan said. "Did you see anything sinister when he left? Or heard anything?"

"I heard a scream," she whispered, looking left and right down the empty hallways. "But I didn't know where it came from. A few minutes later, Mark Tilley emerged from Mrs. Hudson's rooms."

"Did he look odd?" she asked.

"No," Valerie admitted. "But he had a bag of treats with him, and when I checked in on Mrs. Hudson later, she mentioned that he had brought her some snacks to share."

"That is interesting," Meghan muttered to herself. "I wonder if the treats had something in them to hurt Mrs. Hudson."

"What did you say?" Valerie asked. "Are you ready to go in and see Mrs. Sheridan?"

Meghan nodded. "I was just talking to myself," she replied. "And wondering about Mark Tilley. He sounds like an…. interesting...fellow. I'd certainly like to meet him someday."

"Oh?"

Meghan jumped, startled as she felt a tap on her shoulder. Valerie gasped. A tall, broad-shouldered man stood before them with an angry look on his weathered face.

"I'm Mark Tilley," the man growled. "*Why* do you want to talk to *me*?"

8

"MARK TILLEY," MEGHAN STAMMERED as she stared at him. He looked to be about sixty years old, with gray matted hair and a lined face. "First, I am so sorry for your loss."

"What are you doing here, Mr. Tilley?" Valerie asked in annoyance as Mark glowered at her. "I told you over the telephone that Mrs. Hudson's belongings from her suite are not yet available to be collected. You will need to wait until her will is read, and then, only then, you can come retrieve what has been assigned to you."

Mark narrowed his eyes. "Then why is my cousin, Sally Sheridan, allowed to be holed up in my late aunt's suite?"

Valerie frowned. "That is none of your business," she insisted. "Mrs. Sheridan requested not to see you, and we are honoring her wishes at this time. I am going to go fetch security. Meghan?"

Meghan shook her head. "I'll wait here," she told Valerie, who looked at her in shock. "Are you sure?"

Meghan bobbed her head affirmatively. "I'll be fine. And, if Mrs. Sheridan comes to the door, I don't want her to be shocked.

"Your choice," Valerie muttered as she stomped down the hallway.

Meghan stared into Mark's almond-shaped brown eyes. "I'm so sorry for your loss," she said softly.

"What did you say to me?"

"I am so sorry for your loss," she repeated. "It's so difficult to lose someone you care about."

Mark's face fell. "I didn't just care about her," he explained to Meghan. "I loved her. My aunt was the only person who never gave up on me, even after all my troubles. When my own parents, siblings, and cousins turned their backs on me, my Aunt never so much as gave me a harsh word."

Meghan nodded sympathetically. "I am so sorry," she repeated for a third time. "Now...troubles? What do you mean?"

Mark's face twisted in anger. "That's none of your business," he shouted as Meghan gasped. "Who do you think you are?"

"SHE IS MY FRIEND!" Mrs. Sheridan shouted as she threw open the large, heavy door to the suite. "You trashy loser! What do you think you are doing here?"

Mark bared his teeth at his cousin. "That's for me to know," he declared. "You shouldn't be holed up in there, Sally. I was our aunt's favorite. Everything in there belongs to me."

Mrs. Sheridan's face turned red. "Our aunt is dead, and you are worried about collecting what is yours?" she screamed. "You've got some nerve! You filthy, dog-fighting, flea-infested scoundrel! I can't believe your nerve." Mrs. Sheridan stepped forward and spat at Mark. The glob of saliva hit his cheek.

Mark crossed his arms across his broad chest. "That was low, Sally, even for you."

Mrs. Sheridan rolled her eyes. "Boo-hoo, Marky. I bet that hurt your little feelings, didn't it?" she mocked.

Mark's eyes filled with tears, and he turned to storm away. As he walked toward the elevator, an elderly man emerged from his suite. He was short, with round glasses and white hair. "Trouble, folks?" he asked.

Mark glared at the old man. "Mind your own business," he snarled as he pushed past him and banged on the elevator doors. "My auntie never liked you, and she never loved Sally. She never loved anyone like she loved me!"

The elevator doors opened, and Mark dashed inside. As the doors closed, Valerie rounded a corner with three armed security guards. "Is he causing a stir?"

"Yes!" Mrs. Sheridan yelled. "Get him out of here."

Valerie turned to whisper to the guards. They nodded and took off running down the hallway. "So sorry for the disturbance, Mrs. Sheridan," Valerie gushed as she led Mrs. Sheridan back into Mrs. Hudson's suite. Meghan followed, and Valerie turned to wave goodbye to the old man.

"Who was that?" Meghan whispered to Valerie. "Mark yelled at that old man. He said that Mrs. Hudson never liked him."

Valerie sighed. "That was Wayne Rashford," she explained under her breath. "Mark was right...Wayne and Mrs. Hudson had an interesting relationship. But that's not important right now. What is important is getting that monster behind bars! Mark Tilley will never walk into Sevenoaks again, Mrs. Sheridan, I promise!"

9

AFTER THE STRANGE AFTERNOON at Sevenoaks, Meghan returned to the bakery. She was hoping for a normal, quiet afternoon, but as she hung up her jacket, Pamela met her at the back door. "Meghan, I have to show you something," she said grimly.

"What is it?" she asked.

"Pamela retrieved a folder from the bakery's safe. "I've been keeping track of the funeral inquiries, and after getting another Instagram message this afternoon, we are at over one-hundred. I'm getting scared, Meghan."

"I am done with this," Meghan grumbled as she took the folder from Pamela and looked through it. "I don't know if someone out there thinks this is funny, but it isn't. I am going to get to the bottom of this."

Just then, Meghan's phone began to ring. "It's Mrs. Sheridan," she said as she answered the call.

"I need to order a coffin," Mrs. Sheridan said.

"Mrs. Sheridan? It's Meghan Truman. Why are you calling to ask for a coffin?"

Mrs. Sheridan scoffed. "Meghan Truman? You are selling coffins now? That seems like an odd thing to sell at a bakery."

Meghan shook her head. "I'm not selling coffins," she explained. "Why are you calling to ask for one?"

"I found this number online," Mrs. Sheridan told her. "I need to purchase the best possible coffin for my Auntie, and when I looked up "SANDY BAY COFFIN PURCHASE", this was the first number that I found."

"Well, that explains a lot," Meghan muttered. "Someone must have posted the wrong phone number to a funeral website."

"I was trying to call Duly Street, the funeral home," she went on. "I needed to ask them some pricing questions."

"I don't have their number," Meghan said. "But let me look it up." Meghan whipped out her cell phone and typed in the information for Duly Street. "Well, there it is," she murmured. "That is my phone number on the funeral home's website. How did that happen?"

"Do you have their number to give me?" Mrs. Sheridan squawked. "I have a pen and can write it down."

"Let me call you back," she told her. "I have a quick errand to run."

Meghan ran into the dining room to find Trudy and Pamela. "I think I know what the funeral business is all about!" she squealed happily.

"What do you mean?" Trudy asked.

"I'm going to go find out. Ladies, I will be back in a few minutes."

Meghan grabbed her purse and ran out the door toward the Duly Street Funeral Parlor, following the directions she had written down from Trudy. She had never realized there was a funeral parlor only three blocks from her business, and she was happy that Trudy had known where it was located. She knocked on the front door, and a tall, mustached man answered. "Are we expecting you?" he asked.

Meghan shook her head. "No," she replied. "I'm Meghan Truman. I own Truly Sweet, the bakery a few streets over."

The man smiled warmly. "I love your muffins," he gushed as he stuck out his hand to shake Meghan's. "I'm Alfredo Cazale, the owner of the funeral home. Can I help you with something today?"

"I'm having some trouble at my business," she began. "People keep calling to ask for funeral services, and as you know, I run a bakery. We do not offer funeral services. Finally, I realized that the telephone number listed on your website is my telephone number, and that is how people are getting confused."

As he processed Meghan's request, Alfredo brushed his mustache with his fingers, beginning beneath his nose and moving outward. "I'm just not sure I can help you," he shrugged. "I'm not sure what you are really even talking about; you run a bakery. What does that have to do with my funeral parlor?"

Meghan felt her face flush in frustration. "The calls," she explained as she ran a hand through her dark hair. "My bakery has received almost a hundred calls about funeral services. These calls are coming to *me* when they should be going to *you*."

Alfredo's mouth dropped open. "Almost a hundred calls?" he repeated as Meghan nodded. "I've noticed that we have not been getting our normal number of calls this week," he groaned.

"I think your customers have been reaching out to us," she told him. "We thought it was a prank at first, but now, the number of callers and the number of messages we have been receiving has taken up a lot of time and resources. It's affecting my business, and I really want to get to the bottom of things…"

Alfredo's face darkened. "I know what happened," he frowned. "Why don't you come in?"

He led Meghan into a dark parlor. "We don't have any funerals today, so no bodies lying around," he told her as she nervously glanced around. "That elderly woman who passed away at the nursing home is still at the coroner's office, and we won't be expecting her until late this week."

Meghan smiled politely as Alfredo led her to an overstuffed black arm chair. "Have a seat," he graciously told her.

Meghan sat down. "So, do you know what is going on with my website?"

Alfredo nodded. "Yes, I do," he affirmed. "Roberto!"

A teenage boy around Pamela's age came into the room. "Yeah, Dad?"

Alfredo narrowed his eyes at the boy. "Son, remember when I paid you a thousand dollars to reformat our website and to make appropriate updates?"

The boy's brown eyes widened. "Yes?"

Alfredo crossed his arms across his chest. "And did you?"

Roberto nodded. "Yes, of course I did. I worked really hard on it."

Alfredo raised an eyebrow. "Let me see it."

Roberto pulled out his cell phone and gave it to his father. Alfredo handed the phone to Meghan. "Is this your phone number?"

Meghan nodded. "That was what I was talking about! And, now that I'm looking closely, the website looks eerily similar to my website. We just had a designer revamp things, and this almost looks identical to mine."

Alfredo stared at his son. "Did you copy her entire website, Roberto, phone number and all?"

Roberto's lip began to quiver. "Maybe?" he offered. "You offered me the money, and I knew I needed to do the website as fast as I could. I looked at some of the other websites from businesses in town, and hers looked so cool!"

"So you stole the entire website?" Alfredo asked, his face red. "Roberto, what were you thinking?"

"I needed the money for baseball camp," he told his father. "Please, please don't be mad. It was an honest mistake, Pops. I was *inspired* by her website. I swear, I didn't try to *steal* it! "

Alfredo pointed upward. "Go upstairs. I will deal with you later."

Roberto hung his head and walked out of the room, a look of shame on his face. "I am so sorry," Alfredo told Meghan. "I can't imagine the inconvenience this has caused you."

Meghan shook her head. "Honestly, I am just happy that it seems this was a little misunderstanding," she laughed in relief. "It's not a big deal. Teenagers make mistakes, and this is probably a great learning experience for Roberto. Don't be too hard on him."

Alfredo shook his head. "Roberto is a great kid," he explained to Meghan. "He earns straight As, is a star on the baseball team, and he works here several hours a week to earn spending money. I am so proud of that boy. *But!* He is going to certainly learn from this," he assured Meghan. "Mistakes and consequences build character, and Roberto will benefit from this as a learning experience. Since he has wasted your time, he is going to make it up to you. How about he works in your bakery for a few hours this week? He is a good boy and a hard worker, despite the incident with the website, and I think it will be a good way for him to realize that his actions have consequences."

Meghan smiled. "I think that is a great idea," she told him. "He can drop by tomorrow morning, and I will train him."

Alfredo showed Meghan to the door. "Again, my apologies," he told her. "Roberto will be eager to help you tomorrow, I can assure you."

As Meghan left the funeral parlor and waved goodbye to Alfredo, she felt a weight lifted off her shoulders. She now knew who was responsible for the many inquiries, and she was relieved that the intentions had been innocent. Meghan could not wait to tell Pamela, Trudy, and Jack that they had nothing to worry about, and she retrieved her cell phone from her jacket pocket to make a call.

Suddenly, as she stepped onto the street, she saw a blue scarf flying through the air. She hung up her cell phone, stashing it back in her pocket. She lunged for the scarf, groaning as she missed catching it in her left hand. The scarf flew through the air, and Meghan collected her breath as she watched it fly into a green bush outside of the funeral parlor.

Meghan panted, wishing she were in better shape as she slowly walked toward the scarf. "That scarf gave me a run for my money," she breathed as she plucked the faded blue accessory from the bush, careful not to tangle the ends in the leafy branches.

She triumphantly unwound the last piece of the scarf from the bush, and then turned around to find its owner. She spotted someone waving at her from across the square, and she waved back, sure that this person was the owner. Meghan walked toward them, and she could make out the form of an older man sitting on the bench. As she got closer, her heart began to pound; Meghan was dismayed to find that the person waving her over was Mark Tilley, Mrs. Sheridan's least favorite cousin.

"Thank you for bringing my scarf back," Mark Tilley grinned as Meghan's jaw dropped. "It's so good to see you, Meghan."

10

"WHAT ARE YOU DOING HERE?" Meghan asked as she stared at Mark. "Are you following me?"

Mark laughed and shook his head. "Don't flatter yourself," he arrogantly said to her. "I just happened to be out on a walk when I saw you march into the funeral home. I was a little curious about you, especially given that we met just outside of my Auntie's suite. What were you doing at the funeral parlor?"

Meghan shook her head. "That's none of your business," she declared, looking around the streets and hoping someone would be around to hear her scream if she needed to. "I need to go."

"Don't go," he said, reaching to grab Meghan's wrist. "Talk to me for a moment. You said it yourself at the nursing home that you wanted to meet me. Tell me why. Just give me five minutes; I have barely been outside of my house for years. Give an old man some company."

Meghan bit her lip. Mark made her nervous, but she

didn't want to make him angry. She sat down next to him on the park bench, and he smiled brightly. "Thank you," he murmured. "And I wanted to tell you that I am sorry for making the scene at the nursing home. I was frustrated with Sally, and I shouldn't have been rude to that old man."

Meghan looked into his eyes. "Why were you so frustrated with her? I know that things have been...tense...in your family, but you looked extra angry."

Mark sighed. He looked down at the ground. "I was angry," he admitted. "My family history has been complicated, to say the least, and seeing Sally Sheridan at Sevenoaks sent me over the edge."

"What do you mean?" Meghan asked.

"The trouble I was in? What I snapped at you about when you asked me? Well, it's a story that has never been properly told. When I was younger, I was found guilty of running an illegal dog fighting ring, but the truth is that it wasn't me who was in charge of it. It was my Aunt Lucy's husband."

Meghan gasped. "Seriously?" she asked. "Why did you take the fall for him? How did that happen?"

Mark shook his head. "It's complicated," he sighed. "I was just a normal, average young man in Sandy Bay before I got caught up in all of this."

Meghan leaned in. "How did you get into it? Was it your idea?"

Mark chuckled. "I was a skinny little nobody back when this all started," he laughed. "I didn't have the street smarts or resources to start this kind of a hustle. My uncle, Lucy's husband, introduced me to the world of dogfighting."

Meghan's dark eyes widened. "Her husband dragged you into it?"

Mark nodded. "I was a young man looking to make some quick cash, and my uncle told me that he had a way for me to do it. One night, when my aunt was out of town, he told me that we were going to have dinner together at a place just south of town. We drove out of town, and nothing seemed amiss; my uncle and I chatted about the weather, my summer plans, and his upcoming birthday party. I didn't suspect that anything was about to happen."

"And then?" Meghan pried.

"And then, we got to the restaurant. It was a little Italian restaurant fifteen minutes out of town. I had never heard of it. When we walked in, my uncle marched up to the host stand, whispered something into the host's ear, and the guy led us back into a hallway. He knocked on a door, and then, we were led downstairs to the basement."

"The basement?"

Mark nodded. "That's where one of the dog fighting arenas was. I had no idea what was going on, and it wasn't until we left that my uncle fully explained things. He told me that he owned and operated a string of those places, and he wanted me to join the underground family business."

Meghan was shocked. "What did you say?"

Mark looked down at his shoes. "I said yes," he told her. "I needed some money, but I also needed someone to look after me. My own father was pretty cruel to me when I was young, and my uncle seemed like someone I could look up to."

Meghan pursed her lips. "This is crazy," she muttered.

"You have no idea," he sighed. "You should have seen these places; people from all over the world would crowd into these basement areas to watch the shows. You could hear all different languages, see different types of people, and that was just a normal weeknight! On the weekends, my uncle would arrange for the richest, wealthiest people in the industry to come to our arenas. These folks were dripping in dollars. It was the wildest thing I had ever seen."

Meghan shook her head. "If you weren't the mastermind, though, I don't understand how you took the blame," she said to Mark. "This sounds like a seriously complicated situation. Why did you get blamed?"

"His name wasn't connected to any of the accounts," he explained to Meghan. "My uncle traveled a lot, meeting investors, looking for new dogs, and visiting other arenas. When the police finally caught up to us, he was out of town, and they had no idea that he was the hotshot owner of the business. He was instantly acquitted; he wasn't tied to the property in any way, nor was his money invested in it. I, however, was not so lucky; I had thrown my personal funds into the business, and little did I know that because of that, I would be blamed, and my uncle wouldn't even be a suspect."

Meghan raised an eyebrow. "Then why should I believe that he was involved? That all sounds pretty crazy."

Mark buried his face in his hands. "No one ever believes me," he lamented. "Aunt Lucy was mortified when I explained to her what had *really* happened, and she gave my uncle a piece of her mind. She *knew* that I was telling the truth; my aunt always believed in me. She did not believe in losing face, though she knew her husband was responsible for my demise, she did not clear my name."

"Why?" Meghan asked.

"It would have been too humiliating for her," he sighed. "And she said that because I had *some* involvement, I should face some sort of punishment. I took the fall, and she agreed to support me financially until I got back on my feet."

"But you never got back on your feet, did you?" she asked.

"No, I didn't," he confirmed. "After the trial, I was hated in Sandy Bay. No one wanted anything to do with me. I never found a job, I never settled down, and I lived my life dependent on my Aunt's money."

Meghan was shocked by this revelation. She wondered if Mark's story was true. "Why didn't you just leave town?" she asked Mark. "Your reputation here was ruined. Why didn't you start over somewhere new?"

"Trouble always catches up with you," Mark answered matter-of-factly. "People feel so strongly about what they believe I did; animal lovers can be vicious opponents, and I didn't want this kind of a story to follow me to a place where people could hurt me. Staying in Sandy Bay meant that no matter what, I would have protection. My Auntie was untouchable in this town, and while they hated me, they could never do anything to me while she was *alive*. And now, she's gone…."

Mark buried his face in his hands. "I've never forgiven my uncle," he confessed to Meghan. "He let me, a young man, take the fall. At least my Auntie helped me; my uncle never looked my way again, and he treated me like trash even though he was the owner and operator of the dog ring."

Meghan took a deep breath. "That is quite the story," she admitted as they sat quietly on the park bench. "It sounds like you have been through a lot."

"You have no idea," Mark declared.

Meghan's heart sank as she imagined the loneliness of Mark's life. He had no one now that his aunt was gone, and Meghan felt for him. She reached over and took his hand, giving it a squeeze. "I don't know you well, but I want you to know that I am sorry," Meghan said tenderly. "I hope that you will find it in you to move past this, Mark. Forgive your uncle and move on. Being stuck in the past doesn't help anything, and I wish you only the best moving forward."

Mark pulled his hand back from Meghan and glared at her. "Move forward?" he grimaced. "That's a joke. I will never forgive my uncle for setting me up. Never! My uncle was a bad man, and I am still owed a debt from that family. The very least I deserve is every single dime in my aunt's estate, and I won't rest until it is all MINE."

11

MEGHAN WAS SHOCKED as she hurried away from Mark. Things with him had escalated so quickly; she and Mark had been having a perfectly civil conversation, and then, he had grown angry in an instant.

"I was just trying to be a good listener," Meghan thought to herself as she rounded the corner. "He seemed to need someone to talk to, and I was just trying to be a listening ear."

"OUCH!"

Meghan walked right into someone, and she cringed as she felt her body collide with theirs.

"EXCUSE ME!"

Meghan's eyes widened. She found herself staring at Hilda, the owner of the dog grooming parlor.

"I'm so sorry," Meghan apologized as she reached down to collect the lipstick and wallet that had fallen out of Hilda's purse.

"You should watch where you are going," she snapped, bending down to pick up a stray quarter that had fallen onto the sidewalk.

"I didn't even see you coming," Meghan admitted. She saw a piece of paper on the ground, and she picked it up. She turned it over and gasped. It was Lucy Hudson's obituary.

"Give me that," Hilda demanded, holding out her hand.

Meghan held onto the obituary. "Why do you have this?"

Hilda shook her head. "I was friends with Mrs. Hudson. I saw her obituary in the newspaper this morning and cut it out. Not that it is any of your business."

Meghan crossed her arms. "Friends? With a woman that old?"

"She invested in my grooming business," she explained in annoyance. "You know, the grooming business that your jerk boyfriend seemed to hate."

Meghan's face fell. "I'm sorry you heard what Jack said," she said softly. "He is so frugal, and his words came out so rudely. I hope you can forgive him."

Hilda scoffed. "Whatever. I know guys like that: the All-American type who think they are king of the world? He seemed like such a jerk."

Meghan's mouth fell open in shock, but before she could reply, Hilda snatched the obituary out of her hands and stuffed it back inside of her black silk purse. Hilda turned on her heel and marched off down the block.

"Meghan?"

Pamela walked out of the bakery, her face wrinkled in confusion. "Who the heck was that?"

Meghan shook her head. "No one. It was no one."

Later that evening, after Meghan closed the bakery, she decided to go for a walk. Dressed in a chunky white sweater, her running shoes, and a pair of forest-green leggings, she left her apartment and wandered down to the beach, one of her favorite places.

"What a day," she thought to herself as she removed her shoes and walked barefoot along the shoreline. She thought back to her earlier years in Los Angeles. Meghan had moved to Hollywood with dreams of becoming a famous actress, but time after time, she was rejected, never receiving more than a minor role in a soap opera.

As Meghan felt the cool, salty breeze hit her face, she pondered the many times directors and casting managers had dismissed her. With her plucky spirit, Meghan had never been too disheartened, but she imagined that constant rejection, especially from one's own family, could be heartbreaking. She thought of Mark Tilley and his bitterness, how he seemed to be consumed by his anger, and she felt pity for him, as well as curiosity. What would have become of her if *she* had let rejection distract her from happiness during her years in Los Angeles? While she had not become a famous actress, she had made fun memories, gained dear friends, and while she had never achieved her dream of becoming an actress, she had found the silver lining in her life: her rejection had led to the creation of Truly Sweet, her true passion. What could Mark's life have been like had he focused on the good things in his life instead of the heartache?

Meghan walked to the end of the beach, but instead of turning around to venture home, she kept going. She had a lot on her mind, and the walk was a much-needed distraction. After a few minutes she looked up, surprised to find herself at the gates of Sevenoaks.

"I was so lost in my thoughts that I ended up here," she chuckled to herself as she walked up the paved pathway.

As she approached the security station, she heard a car honk behind her. She turned to see a bright red Maserati, the driver waving at her from the front seat.

"Meghan!"

The luxury car rolled up beside Meghan, the window rolled down. Valerie sat behind the steering wheel, her lipstick matching the car's exterior perfectly.

"What a surprise!"

Meghan smiled. "I was on a walk and ended up here,"

she admitted.

"Sounds like you have a lot on your mind," Valerie said.

"It's been a long week," she shrugged. "That's a nice car you have, Valerie. I can smell the leather from here. Is it new?"

Valerie blushed. "I work long and hard," she told Meghan. "I am hardly ever home for dinner with my family, and my husband complains that he doesn't have a wife anymore. I am the breadwinner in my family, and every year, I treat myself to a new car. This year, I had my eye on this little beauty, and now, she is mine."

Meghan giggled. "You are truly embodying the "treat yourself" mentality," she said playfully.

"Work hard, play hard," she agreed. "Hop in, Meghan. I'll drive you up. I'm sure you've never been in a *Mas* before, right?"

"I haven't," Meghan confirmed as she eagerly climbed into the passenger seat. "These seats are so soft!"

"And heated," Valerie chuckled as she pushed a button. "Wait until you turn the radio on; the sound system in this little baby is unmatched!"

Two minutes later, the women arrived in front of Sevenoaks. An attendant dashed out to retrieve the keys from Valerie, and then, the car was driven away.

"Valet parking," she explained to Meghan. "We offer it to our guests, of course."

Valerie marched inside of Sevenoaks. "Mrs. Sheridan is here," she told Meghan. "Would you like to me take you to her? She's been spending some time in our community room; some local church group was here to do crafts with our residents, and Mrs. Sheridan volunteered to clean up their mess. Bless her heart."

Meghan followed Valerie into a large open-concept room. With its high ceilings, bright white walls, and pale blue couches, the aesthetic was clean and crisp, perfectly suited for Sevenoaks. Meghan spied Mrs. Sheridan in a corner, a dust mop in her hand.

"We insisted that she let our staff tidy up," Valerie announced as they walked up to Mrs. Sheridan. "But she wanted to help out."

"It's good to give back," Mrs. Sheridan explained. "My Auntie was quite the philanthropist, and I'm sure she would have wanted me to volunteer here. I should have done it more when she was alive."

Meghan sat down at the light wooden table and patted the seat next to her. "Take a rest?"

Mrs. Sheridan happily complied. "Giving back takes a lot of energy out of me, it seems."

"I'll let you two catch up," Valerie said as she waved goodbye and walked out of the room.

Meghan leaned in. "Speaking of giving back and philanthropy," she whispered to Mrs. Sheridan. "Did your Aunt give back in other ways? Did she ever get involved with businesses?"

Mrs. Sheridan smiled. "She was a proud investor for several of Sandy Bay's startups," she informed Meghan. "She loved empowering young people in business. In fact, I wish I had connected the pair of you when she was alive; she would have loved to help you with the bakery. I wish I had done that."

Mrs. Sheridan hung her head, and Meghan reached over to take her hand. "It's okay," she comforted her. "What kinds of businesses did she invest in?"

Mrs. Sheridan thought for a moment. "She loved animals," she told Meghan. "She loved giving money to different shelters, or to companies that helped animals."

Meghan flashed back to her encounter with Hilda outside of the bakery. "Do you know if she was involved in a new business in town? A pet grooming center?"

Mrs. Sheridan wrinkled her nose. "Doesn't sound familiar. Why do you ask?"

"No reason," Meghan countered. "I was just curious about your aunt. She sounds like an amazing woman."

"She was," Mrs. Sheridan agreed. "Everyone loved her, and she loved everyone. Well, except for that

Wayne Rashford."

"*Who?*"

Mrs. Sheridan frowned. "You're getting a little too curious," she scolded. "It's rude. You should know better manners. I need to leave now, but I hope you think a little harder about being polite the next time we speak. I'm a little disappointed in you."

Mrs. Sheridan gathered her things and flounced out of the room as Meghan stared. Suddenly, she felt a tap on her shoulder.

"I can tell you about Wayne Rashford," said an elderly gentleman.

"I didn't hear you come in. What's your name?" she asked kindly.

The man laughed. "I'm Wayne Rashford," he said jovially. "Nice to meet you."

12

"I THINK IT WAS HILDA," Meghan told Jack as they sipped tea together in the dining room of the bakery. "She is so dark and strange, and the fact that Lucy Hudson invested in her business? Something just seems fishy about her. I think Hilda *definitely* had something to do with it."

Jack took a bite of his carrot cake muffin. "I don't know," he said with a frown. "That seems like a longshot, Meghan. She was mad that I spoke poorly of her grooming business, but I don't think that makes her a killer."

Meghan shook her head. "But she told me herself that Mrs. Hudson was an investor," she argued. "She was so angry when you said those things about her grooming business. What if something happened between her and Mrs. Hudson, and then, she killed her?"

Jack laughed. "You sound crazy," he said to Meghan as he took another bite of his carrot cake muffin. "I just think you are going a little too far with this Hilda thing. What about Wayne? That old man from the nursing home? Didn't you say that he had some weird connection with Mrs. Hudson? What was that about?"

Meghan took a deep breath. She was still rattled from her conversation with Wayne the previous day, and she didn't know where to begin. "It's a long story," she said slowly.

"Go on," he urged her.

"Wayne told me that Lucy killed his twin brother."

Jack's icy blue eyes bulged out of his head. "What did you say?"

Meghan nodded. "Yesterday, at Sevenoaks, he told me that Lucy killed his brother. He said it was an accident; his twin, Dwayne, used to be loud and disruptive around the nursing home. Apparently, Dwayne would leave used tissue paper around, too. Lucy was disgusted by him, and one day, she pushed him down the stairs."

Jack gasped. "Are you serious? Why haven't I heard anything about this at the police station?"

"Mrs. Hudson claimed it was an accident," she shrugged. "She said she didn't mean to push him, and that she lost her own balance and was staggering around. She was so earnest about it that everyone believed her.... everyone but Wayne."

Jack shook his head. "Did Wayne see his brother's fall?"

"No," she said. "Dwayne didn't die instantly; he survived a few more weeks after the fall, but he eventually passed away after a few weeks on painkillers. Wayne said the end was pretty gruesome."

Jack sighed. "What a shame," he said. "It sounds like Mrs. Hudson perhaps wasn't the angel that Mrs. Sheridan believed?"

"I don't know," she admitted. "Wayne had heard that I was spending time with Mrs. Sheridan, Mrs. Hudson's niece, and he wanted to make sure *someone* knew the truth about his brother...or what he believes to be the truth."

Jack bit his lip. "So...do you think Wayne had something to do with Mrs. Hudson's death? I'm going to be honest with you: her death hasn't been filed as a police report yet. The coroner's report is still in progress, but it could be escalated if this were a murder investigation. Do you think that's what we are dealing with, honey?"

Meghan pursed her lips. "I don't know," she said. "Between Hilda and Wayne, there seem to be all sorts of interesting people tied up in Mrs. Hudson's life. And then there is Mark Tilley! What he said to me yesterday on the park bench was chilling, babe. He seems all too keen on receiving the money from Lucy Hudson's estate. What if he took things too far with her? What if she is dead because of his greed?"

Jack frowned. "Meghan," he began gently. "I have to confess: I am a little worried about you. You've taken a serious interest in this situation, and I don't really understand why. You didn't even know Mrs. Hudson, and if we are honest, you aren't particularly close to Mrs. Sheridan. Why are you digging through this one, babe? Is there something more I need to know?"

Meghan crossed her arms and leaned back in her chair. "I'm just tired of people living in the past," she explained. "Mark, Mrs. Sheridan, Hilda, Wayne...all of these people can't move on from the past. If you can't move on from your past, how can you embrace your future? I guess I'm fixated on this situation because it reminds me a bit of how *my* life could have turned out. I faced so much rejection and heartache in Hollywood, but I didn't grow bitter and cynical. I kept going until I found my way. It's just sad that Wayne, Mark, and everyone in this situation seem to be stuck in the past."

Jack nodded. "I knew that you never made it big as an actress," he said as Meghan laughed. "But I didn't realize you experienced that much rejection."

Meghan giggled. "Every single day, babe. The life of a struggling actress is just that--a struggle! It seemed like every other day, someone was slamming a door in my face, denying my portfolio, or refusing to accept my headshots. I became so used to rejection that by the time I left Hollywood to move to Sandy Bay, hearing the word 'no' didn't hurt me anymore."

Jack leaned over and kissed Meghan on the forehead. "You are an inspiration, beautiful," he murmured. "So many people would have been downtrodden from being told no over and over again. You are so positive and upbeat, Meghan! You took all of the rejection and turned it into something amazing--the bakery! I am so proud of you."

Meghan rose from her chair and moved over to sit in Jack's lap. He wrapped his strong, muscular arms around her, and she breathed in the masculine scent of his cologne. "All of my heartache led me here," she said, gently placing a hand on Jack's chest. "I wouldn't trade my life in Sandy Bay for a star on the Hollywood Walk of Fame. I'm happy here. It's all about perspective; finding joy and happiness in the simple things can lead to so much joy, and I wish everyone felt that way. I think Mark's life could have been so much better had he not been stuck in the past…"

Jack brushed Meghan's dark hair aside and kissed her on the cheek. "You are a truly sweet gal," he whispered into Meghan's ear as she cuddled closer to him."

"Eeeewwww!"

Meghan and Jack turned to find Pamela giggling at them in the doorway. "Get a room, you two! Ewww!"

Meghan laughed as she got up from Jack's lap and moved back to her own seat. "Teenagers," she sighed good-naturedly.

"Hey," Jack said as he reached into his backpack and pulled out a Tupperware container. "I have a surprise for you!"

"For me?" Meghan cried in delight as she pried open the container. "It's a muffin!"

Jack grinned. "A homemade muffin. I know you've been busy around here making muffin after muffin, and I wanted to give it a go myself. I made a batch of homemade blueberry muffins last night. They aren't quite up to your standards, but I think they are pretty good. Try them! I substituted yoghurt for butter, and they are so moist."

Meghan laughed as she held the muffin to her nose and inhaled. "It smells good," she gushed. She took a small bite, savoring the taste of the sweet blueberries. "Jack, this is so good," she gushed as she took another bite. "You made this yourself?"

Jack nodded. "I did," he confirmed. "It was a last minute thing, but I wanted to try it. I hope you like it."

"I love it," she cooed as she licked her lips and took another bite. "I'm always baking for everyone else. It's so nice that someone baked for *me.*"

Jack winked at Meghan. "Was it a truly sweet surprise?" he joked as Meghan finished the remainder of the muffin.

"It truly was." she agreed.

13

"I CAN'T BELIEVE HE BAKED FOR YOU,"
Pamela giggled as she, Trudy, and Meghan closed up
the bakery for the evening."

"Jack sure is a keeper," Trudy chuckled.

"He is," Meghan agreed as she wiped the countertop
with a pink rag.

Pamela's phone buzzed, and Meghan watched as the
teenager scrolled through her screen. "Ugh," Pamela
complained. "It's another inquiry for a funeral
service."

"Just have them call Mr. Cazale's office," Meghan
instructed Pamela. "The website at Duly Sweet
Funeral Parlor had our phone number on it, so people
are getting confused. I've spoken with the owner, and
he is working to have it changed. Meanwhile, his son,
Roberto, is going to volunteer here to make up for the
inconvenience."

Pamela's face turned red. "Roberto Cazale?"

Meghan nodded. "He's about your age, isn't he?"

Pamela's face erupted into a smile. "He's a year older than me," she replied dreamily. "He is the most handsome guy at Sandy Bay High School. Meghan, I have been in love with Roberto since I was in fifth grade. Can you schedule me to work with him? Please? I will do anything--clean the bathrooms, scrub the floors, deal with Mrs. Sheridan. Please! Please make sure I get to watch that good looking guy bake cookies?"

Meghan laughed. "Pamela, I've never seen you this way," she remarked in amusement. "You've never struck me as boy crazy. Where is this coming from?"

Pamela stared at Meghan. "Did you not see him?" she asked incredulously. "He is absolutely gorgeous, Meghan."

Meghan recalled Roberto's chubby cheeks and nervous expression. "Ehhhm...sixteen-year olds aren't really my type, but I'm sure he is a nice boy," she told Pamela.

"Just promise you will schedule us together?" she pleaded.

"I'll do my best," Meghan agreed.

The little silver bells at the front door chimed, and Meghan glanced up to see Carl Rainy standing before her. Carl was an officer at the station, and he was a friend of Jack's. Jack had told Meghan that Carl was notorious for researching his cases thoroughly, sometimes to the point of obsession, but Meghan appreciated that he cared about attention to detail. Jack said that Carl was a bit much at times, but everyone at the station knew that if Carl Rainy was on a case, it would inevitably get solved.

"Hey," Meghan greeted him. "What can I do for you, Carl? We're closing a little early tonight; it's been slow today, but we can still get you something."

Carl smiled. "Can I get a box of muffins? Jack let me try some of your matcha muffins last week, and I can't them out of my head."

"Of course!" she agreed. She scurried to the back and grabbed an assortment of muffins. "Here!"

As Meghan handed the box to Carl, she noticed a large purple bruise on his wrist. The bruise was raised, and Meghan shuddered at the gruesome welt. "Carl, what is that? It looks like you got in a wrestling match with a tiger!"

He shook his head. "It's been a long afternoon. That's why I am treating myself with muffins. Long story short, that reclusive nephew of that lady who died? Mark Tilley? He was causing a scene at Winston's bar. I had to arrest him, but he resisted, and here I am, bruised like a peach."

Meghan sighed. "I am so sorry that happened," she lamented. "Here, let me throw in an extra muffin for you. We have a fresh batch cooling now. If you wait ten minutes, I can even send you with two more...maybe three."

"That sounds amazing," Carl agreed. "I'll just wait over there."

Carl meandered to a corner table in the dining room and sat down. As he opened the box and began to eat one of his muffins, Mrs. Sheridan stormed into the bakery.

"Mrs. Sheridan," Meghan greeted. "How are you today?"

Mrs. Sheridan's face was dark. "Not good," she told her. "I received some disturbing news today. My Auntie's report came back from the coroner, and it isn't pretty."

Meghan gasped. "What did it say?"

Mrs. Sheridan wiped a tear from her eye. "The report said that there was a high dosage of some unknown substance in her system."

Meghan's eyes widened. "What? Really? How high?"

Mrs. Sheridan shook her head. "They don't know specifically," she reported. "But they are sure that she had something in her system besides her normal medications. They aren't absolutely sure that that is why she passed away, but if you ask me, it sounds fishy. I think we have a murder on our hands. A murder!"

Meghan gave Mrs. Sheridan a hug "I am so sorry to hear that," she told the older woman. "What can I do to help, Mrs. Sheridan? I feel so badly that this is happening."

Mrs. Sheridan produced a monogrammed handkerchief from her handbag and blew her nose. "I don't know what to do next," she admitted. "But I think I know who killed her!"

"Who would that be?"

Mrs. Sheridan narrowed her eyes. "Mark Tilley, that no-good-for-nothing cousin of mine," she spat. "He has been trouble since he was a young man, and I believe he wouldn't think twice about killing off our Auntie. She has been nothing but good to him, but he has a wicked heart. I'm sure that he is responsible. Even Valerie Hodge agrees! She told us he was at the nursing home on the night before Auntie died. I would bet my life that he had something to do with this."

Meghan bit her lip. "It sounds like you have a lot to think about right now," she murmured to Mrs. Sheridan. "Why don't I pack up some goodies for you, and then Trudy can take you home? You need your rest, especially after this stressful news."

Mrs. Sheridan nodded. "That sounds good."

Meghan went to find Trudy, who was in the kitchen. "Can you take Mrs. Sheridan home?" she asked. "She's wandered in, and she is quite upset."

Trudy nodded. "No problem. But Meghan? We had another call for the funeral home."

Meghan sighed. "Just direct them to the real funeral parlor, please."

Trudy shook her head. "It came from a woman named Valerie," she told Meghan. "Wasn't the director at Sevenoaks named Valerie? It was a weird call. She called and emailed several times about funeral services. She listed an incredibly high price and asked for the funeral home to expedite the preservation process."

"Preservation process?"

"Of the body," Trudy explained. "It was a ton of money, Meghan. I've never seen so many zeros. Anyway, since you know her, would you mind giving her a call back while I drop off Mrs. Sheridan?"

"I can do that," Meghan agreed. "I'll call her back as soon as I run these muffins out to Carl."

Meghan waved goodbye to Mrs. Sheridan and Trudy, and then took the box of fresh muffins to Carl. "Sorry it took so long," she apologized. "We had more of that funeral business again."

"Funeral business?"

Meghan nodded. "Our phone number was accidently placed on the local funeral parlor's website, and we've been getting all sorts of calls about funeral services. We just had one from Valerie Hodge, the director of the nursing home. I need to call her back and let her know that she's been contacting the wrong business. We don't do funeral services at this bakery."

Carl laughed. "Such a strange situation. Hey, speaking of the nursing home, I overheard Mrs. Sheridan's concerns about her late aunt's death. It sounds like a strange situation. I'm wondering if perhaps I need to file a police report, especially given the dynamic with that Mark Tilley. Since you know the nursing home director personally, would you mind mentioning the idea to her when you give her a call?"

Meghan smiled. "I was thinking about just going over there myself," she told Carl. "Why don't you come along? She's so elegant and hospitable, and the nursing home is so fancy."

Carl nodded. "Sure, I can do that."

Carl and Meghan went to Carl's car. As Meghan buckled in, she glanced over at Carl, who was eating another muffin. "Is it good?"

"The best," Carl confirmed as he turned on the car. "Gosh, I know you said that the nursing home is nice, but can you imagine working with so many old people? That poor Valerie must have to work with funeral homes all of the time. How depressing."

"That would be a challenge," she agreed as they pulled away from the bakery. "I wouldn't love that part of the job."

Carl turned toward the nursing home. "Tell me more about this aunt of Mrs. Sheridan," he said. "What was she like?"

Meghan bit her lip. "She was...interesting," she answered, wanting to be diplomatic in the way she discussed the deceased. "I didn't know her personally, but I hear she was a spitfire."

"Sounds like Mrs. Sheridan," he replied.

"I know that she was loved, but not always necessarily liked," she told him.

"Again, sounds like Mrs. Sheridan," he laughed as they checked in at the security booth.

The security guard directed them to the front entryway of the nursing home, and a uniformed attendant came to the window. "I can take your keys for valet parking, sir."

"Valet parking?" Carl chuckled. "This is five-star treatment, huh? Look, buddy, I'm not allowed to let anyone else drive my squad car, so I will have to park it myself."

"As you wish," the attendant said. "The parking garage is underground. You can follow me to the entrance."

After Carl parked, they exited the police car and walked into the airy foyer. "This is insane," Carl remarked as he looked around the nursing home. "All of this for the old people? It looks like I need some gray hairs on my head to get the star treatment."

Meghan smiled. "I think it's nice," she told him. "It's nice that the elderly residents of Sandy Bay have a nice place to live out their days."

Just as they approached the check-in desk, Valerie Hodge greeted them. "Meghan! What a pleasure," she called out. "The guards let me know that you were here. To what do I owe this surprise?"

Meghan gestured at Carl. "This is my friend, Officer Rainy," she explained. "He has a few questions for you, and I also wanted to chat."

Valerie nodded politely. "Of course," she said. "Right this way. My office is being painted, but we can chat in the conservatory."

14

THE TRIO ARRIVED IN THE CONSERVATORY, a large, elegant room with a grand piano in the corner. A fire roared in a marble fireplace adjacent to the piano, and Meghan marveled at the grandeur of the room. A lone figure was sitting in a white leather chair by the window, and Valerie waved casually as she led them inside. "Hi, dear. How are you doing today?"

Meghan's palms grew sweaty as she realized the lone figure was Hilda. She bit her lip. "Who is that?" she quietly asked Valerie, not wanting to cause a scene.

"That's Hilda," Valerie explained with a smile as Hilda glared at Meghan and then left the room. "Her father used to live here, and her uncle currently is one of our darling residents. Hilda drops by every once and awhile. She says that being here helps her feel closer to her deceased father."

Meghan's heart pounded. "Who is her uncle?" she asked.

"I believe you've met him," she said. "Wayne

Rashford? His brother was Hilda's father."

Meghan felt her stomach churn. "Can I ask you a weird question?" she asked Valerie as they walked across the conservatory. "Did Hilda know Lucy Hudson?"

Valerie nodded. "She did. I used to see the pair of them chatting on occasion. In fact, I think Hilda was one of Mrs. Hudson's last visitors before she died."

Meghan's face paled as Valerie led them to a sitting area comprised of two leather sofas and a tall gray armchair. She sat down and gestured for them to sit as well. "Now, what can I do for you today, Officer?"

Meghan noticed that Valerie looked weary. She herself had felt apprehensive at first when she was in the beginning of her relationship with Jack; it was strange to be around people in uniform all of the time, and she wondered if Valerie was intimidated by Carl's tall stature and police attire.

Carl smiled. "Thank you for having us in this nice room. This whole place is so fancy."

Valerie smiled and sat taller in her seat. "I pride myself on providing the highest quality care and experience for my clients," she boasted. "I appreciate your kind words."

Before Carl could continue the conversation, Wayne Rashford walked into the room. "I heard you were here," he shouted as he pointed to Meghan.

"Hi, Wayne," Meghan greeted. "How are you?"

Wayne shook his head. "I hope that Mrs. Sheridan isn't with you today," he announced. "Because I'm glad that her aunt, that old bat, is dead!"

At that moment, Mrs. Sheridan walked into the room. "That was so rude!" she screeched as Wayne's face paled. "How dare you? Get out of here."

Valerie leapt to her feet. "Mr. Rashford!" she chided. "That is impolite. We should not speak of the deceased in such a way."

Meghan raised an eyebrow at Mrs. Sheridan. "What are you doing here?" she asked her as Mrs. Sheridan joined her on the couch.

Mrs. Sheridan licked her lips. "Valerie called me. She said I was free to pick up my Auntie's things from her suite. I just arrived, and the front desk attendant told me that she was up here meeting with you."

Valerie stood to shoo Wayne out of the room, and Meghan noticed Carl had taken out a pad of paper. "For some notes," he whispered to her as Valerie rejoined them. "That encounter seemed suspicious."

Valerie sat down and folded her hands over her lap. "I apologize for his outburst," she said with sad eyes. "Wayne seems to be...not well."

Carl shrugged. "It's okay," he told her. "Anyway, Valerie, let me be frank: I have some concerns regarding the death of Lucy Hudson, and I am interested in filing a report."

Mrs. Sheridan's eyes widened. "You were in the corner at the bakery when I stopped by."

Carl nodded. "I was," he confirmed. "And I overheard your concerns. I decided to stop by and talk with Mrs. Hodge here about your Auntie. What a perfect coincidence that you showed up."

Mrs. Sheridan smiled. "I'm glad you are here. I want to get to the bottom of this, Valerie. The report from the coroner was disturbing, and I want more information."

Valerie bobbed her head in agreement. "I understand that you are upset," she said soothingly, reaching over to pat Mrs. Sheridan's hand. "But with patients as old as your aunt, sometimes, these things just happen. Medications can affect them differently, or sometimes, their medications stop working."

Mrs. Sheridan bit her lip. "But it all just seems odd," she protested. "I want more information, and I think I have a right to it, don't I?"

Carl agreed. "You do," he said.

Valerie rose from her seat. "No problem, then. We can get you all of the information you would like."

Valerie turned to leave the room, but then came back to the group. "Meghan? So sorry, but didn't you want something as well? I am going to go pull all of Mrs. Hudson's files, but before I go….?"

Meghan smiled. "I just wanted to clear up the emails," she told Valerie. "You accidentally emailed the bakery about funeral services, and I wanted to let you know that you needed to touch base with the funeral parlor instead."

Valerie's face paled. "Oh," she murmured. "I'm not sure what you are talking about."

Meghan shook her head. "You called, too. Trudy said you were looking into some expensive funeral services? You wanted to expedite the burial process?"

Mrs. Sheridan cocked her head to the side. "Whose? Whose burial process were you trying to expedite, Valerie?"

Suddenly, a maid appeared at Valerie's side. "Mrs. Hodge? A special package has arrived for you."

Valerie excused herself for a moment. "I'll just go get those files and see about that package. I won't be but a moment."

"Wait!" Carl ordered, but it was too late; Valerie was long gone.

"She was acting shifty," Mrs. Sheridan announced as Carl rose to his feet. "She's hiding something. I can tell."

Carl put away his notepad and pulled out his walkie-talkie. "I agree," he said to the group. "Something is going on here, and I am calling for backup."

A moment later, an alarm went off. Meghan, Carl, and Mrs. Sheridan hustled out of the conservatory. "It must be a fire," Meghan yelled as they took the stairs to the first floor and left the building. Dozens of other patients were fleeing as well, with maids and butlers assisting them.

"It wasn't a fire," Mrs. Sheridan whispered as they exited the building. "Look!"

Everyone gasped. Near the security booth, they could see a lopsided red Maserati with smoke coming out of it. "That's Valerie's car!" Meghan exclaimed as more residents poured from every exit of the building.

"Help! Help!"

Everyone turned to find Wayne Rashford laying on the pavement. He was cradling his leg, a pained look in his eyes. "She hit me," he gasped as blood poured from his wound. "Valerie Hodge hit me with that fancy car of hers!"

15

"SHE WAS RESPONSIBLE for how many murders?!"

Meghan and Jack walked arm and arm along the beach. It was the first time they had seen each other in two days; Jack had been consumed with the Valerie Hodge case, and this was his first break in forty-eight hours.

"Five in total," he said as a cool gust of wind stung their faces, sending Meghan's wavy hair flying. "Valerie Hodge is wanted in three states for the murder and abuse of the elderly."

Meghan shook her head. "But she said she had lived in Sandy Bay for years," she told Jack. "She worked her way up at Sevenoaks."

"True," Jack admitted. "She committed the other murders when she was a young woman. From what we've found, she was nearly caught in Indiana. She hightailed it out of the Midwest and ended up here, slowly working her way up at the nicest nursing home in the Pacific Northwest."

Meghan gasped. "What a con artist!" she cried. "She seemed so elegant and put-together. I can't believe she tricked us all."

Jack shook his head. "We were stunned at the station when we pieced it all together," he explained. "Valerie Hodge manipulated her elderly patients into making her the sole beneficiary of their wills. Mrs. Hudson was no exception; I've spoken with her attorney, and it looks like last month, she had her will changed to name Valerie as the beneficiary."

"Right before she died," Meghan murmured.

"Yep. Except it looks like the paperwork was forged," Jack said. "Her attorney thought it was odd, but there was nothing she could do; she was sworn to a confidentiality agreement."

Meghan bit her lip. "How sad," she said. "So will Mrs. Sheridan and Mark receive anything from Mrs. Hudson's estate?"

Jack shrugged. "We're still working on that with her attorneys," he sighed. "But I think we will be able to work it out."

They walked along, both enjoying the feeling of the sand between their toes. It was a warm day, and Meghan loved the way the sun shone in the sky after the long winter.

"So how did you catch her?" she asked. "At the nursing home, when they checked out the smoking car, she was long gone."

Jack laughed. "Somehow, that woman in her high heels made it to the border," he told Meghan. "She was trying to buy a bus ticket at a stop near northern California, and one of our guys picked her up."

Meghan stopped in her tracks. She turned to gaze at the dark, stormy waters of the Pacific Ocean. "I just can't believe Valerie turned out to be such a monster."

"She really was," he confirmed. "The autopsy report stated that she died from a lethal injection. We found evidence of drugs and needles in Valerie's office, so we have all of the evidence we need."

Meghan wrinkled her nose. "I just can't believe that Hilda had nothing to do with any of this mess," she told Jack. "I feel embarrassed that I judged her so harshly. I was convinced that she had something to do with Mrs. Hudson's death. You should have seen me at the nursing home, Jack! When we walked into the conservatory and I learned that Hilda was the daughter of Wayne's brother, the one that Mrs. Hudson didn't get along with, I nearly vomited. It just seemed to me like she was so entangled in Mrs. Hudson's story that she had to be involved."

Jack nodded. "It's a strange feeling to find out that someone you thought was guilty is innocent," he admitted as he waved a seagull away from his head. "It happens with cases I work on, and it is a disconcerting feeling. It just goes to show that it is so important to have evidence and not solely rely on feelings."

Meghan frowned. "I think I want to do something nice for Hilda," she told Jack. "I feel like the three of us got off on the wrong foot, and I want to make things right. I think I might invite her over for dinner next week. From what I know, she doesn't have any family left in town; I've heard that her mother and sisters moved away when their father died, and I think it could be nice for her to know some friendly faces."

Jack pulled Meghan close to him and gave her a squeeze. "How are you such a sweetheart?" he asked her as she smiled up at him.

"It's the right thing to do," she told her boyfriend. "Plenty of people supported me as I moved to Sandy Bay and opened my business, and she's in the same boat—alone with a new business to run. Maybe we can even become friends."

Jack laughed. "You manage to make friends with everyone," he said proudly. "Speaking of your friends, how is Sally Sheridan doing these days?"

Meghan pursed her lips. "Poor Mrs. Sheridan," she said. "First, she lost her aunt, and now, a murder scandal? It's too much for an older woman to bear."

Jack took Meghan's hand and gave it a squeeze. "You are so worried about her," he murmured. "You have the biggest heart, Meghan. That's one of the things I love most about you."

Meghan smiled up at Jack. "I just want the best for the people I love."

"So you're saying that you love grumpy old Mrs. Sheridan?" he teased.

Meghan giggled. "I don't know about love, but I do care about her."

Jack swept Meghan into a hug as another heavy gust of wind hit them. "So...if you don't love Mrs. Sheridan, who do you love?"

Meghan cast her eyes up at her handsome boyfriend. "You know that I love you, babe," she whispered into Jack's ear as he ran a hand through her long, messy hair.

Jack leaned down toward Meghan. He pulled his hands from her waist and placed them on her red cheeks. Meghan tilted her head upward, closing her eyes sighing as they kissed. "I love you, Meghan," Jack breathed as he went in for another slow, deep kiss.

They stood together on the shoreline for several minutes, both reveling in the peaceful moment away from town as the sun set over the horizon. The evening was brisk, but beautiful, and both Meghan and Jack were trying to take in the lovely moment.

Finally, Meghan looked down at her silver watch and sighed. "I have to go," she told Jack. "I left Pamela and Roberto at the bakery, and Trudy's shift ends soon."

"Roberto?"

"He's the son of the funeral parlor owner, Alfredo Cazale. Roberto is helping out at the bakery for a bit. He started with some baking, but now, I'm having him do a few things on our website. He's not too bad at web design, and I've seen our internet traffic spike since he took control of our Facebook page. Pamela also has a huge crush on him, and the two of them make these big, flirty eyes at each other all of the time."

"Like *us*?" Jack flirted as Meghan blushed.

"Yes, like us. I need to run, babe; Trudy is leaving, and I can't trust those two alone together. I need to get back and chaperone the teenage love birds."

Jack put a hand on Meghan's shoulder. "Sounds good, but before you go, let's take another minute here together. This night is perfect, just like you, and I want to soak it in."

Meghan nodded, placing an arm around Jack's waist. "It is perfect," she agreed. "It is truly sweet."

The End

Afterword

Thank you for reading Muffins and Coffins! I really hope you enjoyed reading it as much as I had writing it!

If you have a minute, please consider leaving a review on Amazon.

Many thanks in advance for your support!

About King Cake and Grave Mistakes

Released: January, 2019
Series: Book 11 – Sandy Bay Cozy Mystery Series
Standalone: Yes
Cliff-hanger: No

A spate of muggings. A murdered victim. Can a small town bakery owner solve the case before the killer ending?

Meghan Truman has cornered the desserts market in the Pacific Northwest. With her twin poodles by her side, the once-upon-a-time newbie in town is set to grow her mini empire. But Meghan has a real-life murder mystery on her hands when a pampering party for a famous painter ends with the demise of a guest.

How could a girly night of fun and laughter with some tasty nibbles end on such a sour note?

As Meghan continues her investigation, she discovers one common denominator links all the suspects on her list: their relationship to the famous painter...plus their consumption of her king cake!

With her boyfriend, handsome detective Jack Irvin out of town, will Meghan discover the mistakes the killer made to link them to the murder?

KING CAKE AND GRAVE MISTAKES
CHAPTER 1 SNEAK PEEK

IT WAS A DULL, DARK EVENING in January, and twenty-seven year old Meghan Truman was fighting a serious case of the winter blues. Nearly three weeks into the New Year, the novelty of the holiday season had worn off, and Meghan's life in Sandy Bay, a small town in the Pacific Northwest, felt drab and dreary. Meghan's professional life was booming; as the sole owner of Truly Sweet, a quaint bakery that had gained enormous popularity over the last few months, Meghan could hardly keep up with the incoming requests for treats, and the new sets of corporate orders seeming to pour in each day.

"I need to do something to perk myself up," Meghan thought to herself as she scrubbed the front counter of the bakery. "I've felt down in the dumps for the last few days. I wish I could call Jack."

Meghan's heart sank at the thought of her tall, handsome boyfriend, Jack Irvin. With his blonde hair and bright blue eyes, Meghan swooned every time she looked at him. Jack was a detective, and for the next two weeks, he was out of town in New Orleans for a special training. Meghan had anticipated his time away would feel fast; her schedule was so busy, and she hardly had time for herself. Yet, while Jack had been gone for only two days, it had felt like two years.

Meghan glanced out at the gloomy night. The thick snow covering the town had melted into a gray mess, and the bitter winter sea gusts cut through Meghan's coat every time she stepped outside. She longed for the mild winters of Los Angeles, the city she had lived in before moving to Sandy Bay, and even more, she desperately ached for the hot, humid winters of Texas, the state where she had grown up.

Suddenly, Meghan looked over at the bulletin board next to the rack of aprons and was struck with inspiration. Pinned to the board was a pamphlet from the salon in town, owned by her good friend, Jackie. Meghan remembered that Jackie was hosting late-night salon hours this week as a January special, and she grinned. She had sent her employees home hours ago, and after finishing her preparations for the next day, Meghan knew it was time to leave the bakery for the night. She looked down at her hands. Meghan's palms were calloused from hours of kneading dough, her fingers had small abrasions from dicing fruit, and her cuticles were wild and overgrown. "I know what I'm going to do," Meghan exclaimed as she examined her rough hands. "I'm going to get a manicure at Jackie's. I'll be right in time to catch her late night hours, and my hands could use some pampering. Everyone is gone for the night, my work is finished, and I think it's time to take care of myself.

Twenty minutes later, Meghan skipped into the Sandy
Bay salon owned by her good friend, Jackie. Meghan
hadn't dressed up and had hastily thrown her long,
dark hair into a messy bun, unaware of how upscale
Jackie's clientele would be. It wasn't until she looked
down at the floor in the waiting area and saw designer
bag after designer bag perched next to their
glamorous owners.

"Maybe I should have showered before leaving the
bakery," Meghan thought as she peered at the other
guests lounging in the waiting area. "That woman is
dripping in jewelry, and that man over there has shoes
that must have cost him a fortune. I hope I don't
embarrass Jackie with my messy hair and sweatpants;
it looks like the people in here are way fancier than I
expected."

Meghan fidgeted in her seat as she surveyed the
waiting area. The spacious room was lit by three
sparkling chandeliers, and the white tile floors were
covered with Persian rugs. A fountain in the corner
held several large, exotic-looking fish, and the
receptionist's desk was made from what appeared to
be crystal.

"Jackie never mentioned how nice this place has
gotten," Meghan grumbled as a lithe, blonde woman
glided into the salon.

"Meghan!"

Meghan smiled weakly as Jackie appeared. "Thanks
for squeezing me in, Jackie," Meghan told her friend
as Jackie kissed her on both cheeks. "The salon looks

amazing, Jackie. When did it become so classy?"

Jackie shrugged. "My internet-based business coach, Donna, suggested that I spruce things up a little," she explained to Meghan. "Donna thinks I should create an atmosphere for the clients I want, and the clients I want have a lot of money," she whispered to Meghan. "During the holidays, I had some spare time, and I decided to do a little shopping to make this place shine."

Meghan's eyes widened. "It looks like you did more than a little shopping," she laughed nervously as Jackie led her back to the manicure room. "This place looks so nice. I don't think I'm dressed well enough to even breathe the air here, Jackie."

Jackie shook her head. "Enough of that kind of talk, Meghan," she chided. "You are a friend of mine, and you belong here. Come sit! I have just enough time to give you a fabulous new color and nail shape before my next appointment arrives. Oh, Meghan, I am so glad you called. I've been dying to get my hands on your nails."

"This is just what I needed," Meghan admitted as she settled into the plush red chair in front of the manicure station.

"Good," Jackie agreed as she glanced down at her rose gold watch. "Yikes. Meghan, I have another client scheduled for eyelash extensions that I completely forgot about. I'm going to have my two assistants start taking care of you. Dolly? Polly?"

Two identical brunette girls appeared by Jackie's side. They looked young--Meghan guessed they were in their early twenties--and Meghan could not tell them apart.

"Meghan, these are my assistants, Dolly and Polly. They are new to the salon, but I hope they give you the best experience. I know they will, right girls?"

The two girls nodded, and Meghan smiled warmly at them. "It's fine,' she told Jackie. "We'll be fine."

Jackie scurried off, and Dolly lifted Meghan's left hand into a small silver bowl while Polly moved Meghan's right hand into a matching silver bowl. They worked in sync, both moving and breathing at the same pace. Meghan was mesmerized by their precision, and she stared as the twins pampered her.

"Meghan? You doing okay?"

Meghan's body jerked as she heard Jackie's voice. She realized she had been sleeping; she was so relaxed as the twins did her nails that she had drifted off to sleep.

"I'm good," she sleepily said to Jackie. "This is so cozy; the twins are doing a great job."

"What color did you pick?" Jackie asked.

Polly held up a bottle of the Josie Posie polish. "She selected this Josie Posie pink," Polly told Jackie.

"I think Jack will like it," Meghan gushed. "He

always compliments me when I wear pink."

Jackie winked. "I think you're right. Ugh, Meghan, I have to run. I have to get over to the other manicure station. One of my clients is being a little...demanding...so I am going to go relieve my other assistant. I just wanted to check on you."

Meghan grinned. "Hey, I'm an easy client," she joked with her friend. "Just let the twins take care of me, and I will float on out of here."

Meghan smiled at the twins as Jackie flew away. "I really miss my boyfriend," she confided in them. "He's been gone a few days, and I'm a little lonely."

Before the twins could respond, Meghan heard a screech. "Seriously? You seriously think it is acceptable to leave my nails looking like that? This color is atrocious. It looks like a circus clown stuck his hands into a tomato patch. I can't believe this is the quality of the service here."

Meghan looked over her shoulder to see Jackie forcing herself to smile. "Rosie, my assistant simply didn't pair the color correctly. I am happy to give you a new color and comp it. My treat."

Meghan raised an eyebrow. Rosie, the woman who had screeched, looked glamorous. She had sharp features, with a pointed nose and bold jawline, and white blonde hair cut bluntly just above her collarbone. She was dressed in white leather pants, a black cashmere turtleneck, and matching white heeled boots.

"I don't have the time to wait for another color, Jackie," Rosie complained. "I'm meeting my boss for dinner in twenty minutes."

Meghan watched as Jackie bent down beside Rosie and began to work. "Just give me ten minutes, Rosie, and I'll have you out of here."

True to her word, ten minutes later, Rosie was beaming and kissing Jackie on the cheek as she rose from her chair and examined her nails. "Thank you, I owe you one," Rosie cooed as Jackie grinned.

"It's really no problem," Jackie assured Rosie as she escorted her to the waiting area. "I apologize my assistant did not deliver on the color you desired."

"Well, you fixed it so promptly that I have nearly forgotten all about it," Rosie said with a wink. "But really, I owe you one, Jackie. I'll see you next week for my appointment."

As Rosie sashayed out the door of the salon, Meghan gestured for Jackie to come over. Meghan's hands were deep in a dryer, and she was eager to hear about Jackie's customer. "Who was that?" Meghan asked. "Is she local? I've never seen her in town before."

Jackie rolled her eyes. "She's the personal assistant to someone important...I have to admit though, I've always tuned her out whenever she starts bragging about her job.

Meghan nodded. "Got it. She seemed like a real piece of work," she said.

Jackie laughed. "You have no idea."

Later that evening, after Jackie closed up the salon, she asked Meghan if she would run some errands with her. "We haven't gotten to catch up since New Year's," Jackie lamented. "Hop in my car and chat with me. I only have a few places to go, and it would be nice to have someone to talk with."

Meghan agreed, and she accompanied Jackie on her errands. They visited the grocery, the pharmacy, and the library, happily chatting as they made their purchases.

"Can I ask you a question?" Jackie asked as they headed toward the post office.

"Of course," Meghan replied.

Jackie took a deep breath. "How did you really get your business off of the ground, Meghan?"

Meghan cocked her head to the side. "What do you mean?"

Jackie bit her lip. "Well, things are on the up and up with the salon, but I want to really rock it. How did you do it with your bakery? Things were slow for you, and then they just took off."

Meghan shrugged. "It was the corporate orders," she admitted. "I love serving the people of Sandy Bay, but when I started catering for several of the big companies, I really saw the dollar pour in."

Jackie nodded. "I'm hoping some slam dunk client wanders in sooner than later," she sighed. "Someone rolling in the dough, you know?"

Jackie slammed on the brakes. "Hey!" she screamed, narrowly avoiding a pedestrian who had darted in front of the car. "Watch where you are going."

Meghan's heart was pounding. "What was she doing?"

Jackie glared as the female pedestrian scurried inside of the post office "People are so careless. She was probably on her phone, distracted."

Both women unbuckled their seatbelts, Meghan's heart still beating rapidly as Jackie turned off the car.

"Last stop," Jackie declared. "This will be a quick stop, I promise."

As Meghan and Jackie walked into the post office, Meghan gasped. "Jackie," she whispered. "Isn't that Rosie? From the salon?"

"Oh goodness," Jackie muttered. "It is. We have to say hi, even though I don't feel like dealing with her again."

"Darling Jackie!"

Meghan watched Jackie paste a smile on her face as

Rosie spotted Jackie.

"Hello, Rosie," Jackie said. "Good to see you."

Meghan noticed a woman in sunglasses behind Rosie. The woman had waist-length sandy hair, and wore a long pink coat. She was curvy, and her expensive outfit made her look womanly and beautiful. It was the same woman who had darted in front of Jackie's car only moments before.

"Jackie, Jackie's friend, this is the esteemed Mariah Cooper," Rosie said as the woman in sunglasses nodded at them. "She is an artist, and my dearest friend."

Meghan watched as Jackie's jaw dropped. "Mariah Cooper? The Mariah Cooper?"

Mariah Cooper pushed her sunglasses atop her head and nodded. "Yes, Mariah Cooper," she said coolly. "I believe you almost ran me over out there?"

"I...I....I'm so sorry," Jackie sputtered. "I didn't realize it was you."

Meghan saw the desperation in Jackie's face. Hoping to ease the tension, she smiled and reached out her hand. "Nice to meet you," she said. "I'm Jackie's friend, Meghan. Mariah, I hear you are a great painter and sculptor."

Mariah turned up her nose as Rosie shook her head. "She isn't just a great painter and sculptor," Rosie informed Meghan. "Her work is iconic. She is only twenty-seven years old, and her work is being featured at the Winter Olympics next year. She is internationally acclaimed."

Meghan playfully shrugged. "Does she ever speak for herself?"

Rosie's jaw dropped. "I don't think you understand," she said dismissively. "Mariah doesn't just talk to anyone. She is famous."

Jackie gently pushed Meghan behind her. "Meghan is just being silly," she said apologetically. "She is a jokester. Anyway, Rosie, Mariah, it was a pleasure. We must be going."

As Jackie and Meghan walked out of the post office, Jackie hissed at Meghan. "You could have jeopardized my business with Rosie with your sass."

Meghan bit her lip. "I was just trying to get them to get over themselves," she said. "I know that type, and they seemed so stuck up."

Jackie scowled. "That wasn't your place. You should just play it good next time, Meghan, if you know what's good for you. Mariah Cooper could be that slam dunk client I've been hoping for!"

You can order your copy of **King Cake and Grave Mistakes** at any good online retailer.

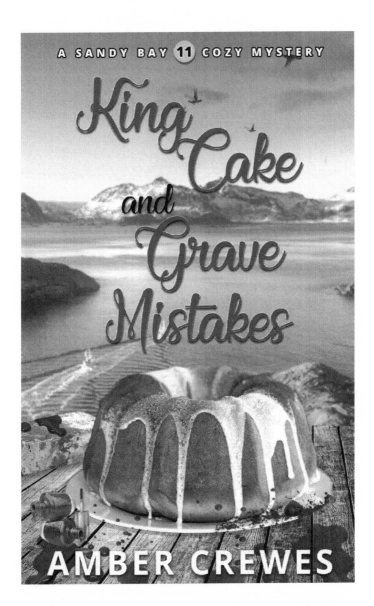

A SANDY BAY **11** COZY MYSTERY

King Cake and Grave Mistakes

AMBER CREWES

ALSO BY AMBER CREWES

The Sandy Bay Cozy Mystery Series

Newsletter Signup

Want **FREE** COPIES OF FUTURE **AMBER CREWES** BOOKS, FIRST NOTIFICATION OF NEW RELEASES, CONTESTS AND GIVEAWAYS?

GO TO THE LINK BELOW TO SIGN UP TO THE NEWSLETTER!

www.AmberCrewes.com/cozylist

Amber Crewes

Muffins and Coffins

Manufactured by Amazon.ca
Bolton, ON